"What did you feed them for lunch?" Kaitland demanded.

She set Maddie down and gathered Bobby to her.

"Cookies," Max quietly admitted. "And milk."

"That's all?" Kaitland's eyes widened.

"They seemed to like it," he added defensively.

Cradling a child in each arm, Kaitland shook her head. "It's nap time. I need to put them down, and then we'll talk about their schedule."

"Their schedule? You make them sound like army recruits."

"You really don't know anything about babies, do you?"

Max ran a weary hand through his hair. "You know I don't. But I've sent for someone from the agency at the church. They've assured me that…" His eyes suddenly narrowed. "Which brings me back to my original question, Kaitland. What are *you* doing here?"

"Surprise," Kaitland said brightly. "I'm the new nanny."

Books by Cheryl Wolverton

Love Inspired

A Matter of Trust #11
A Father's Love #20

CHERYL WOLVERTON

Growing up in a small military town in Oklahoma where she used to make up stories with her next-door neighbor, Cheryl says she's always written, but never dreamed of having anything published. But after years of writing her own Sunday school material in the different churches where she's taught young children, and wanting to see more happy endings, she decided to give it a try and found herself unable to stop.

Seeing so many people hurting, afraid to reach out and accept God's forgiveness, inspired her to begin writing stories about God's love and forgiveness in romances, because, she says, "We can't truly have happily ever after, if we don't have that happily-ever-after relationship with God, too."

Cheryl now lives in a small Louisiana town and has been happily married for fifteen years. She has two wonderful children who think it's cool to have a "writing mama." Cheryl would love to hear from her readers. You can write to her at P.O. Box 207, Slaughter, LA 70777.

A Father's Love
Cheryl Wolverton

Published by Steeple Hill Books™

STEEPLE HILL BOOKS

Steeple Hill™

ISBN 0-373-87020-5

A FATHER'S LOVE

Copyright © 1998 by Cheryl Wolverton

Trust in Him in all things. Pour out your heart
before Him. God is our refuge.

—Psalms 62:8

Wow. A second book. And so many people to thank. My GEnie pals: Kathi Nance, Judy DiCiano, Shannon Lewis and Nancy aka Igor; and Yvonne Grapes, my mail critique partner. And Gayle Anderson who willingly read over this for mistakes. They are wonderful to bounce ideas off of.

And of course Jean Price, my agent, and Anne, my editor, who both have been unfailingly patient with me as I learn the process of just what goes into publishing a book. And Anita Slusher and Debbie Weaver.

But most of all, my daughter, Christina, my son, Jeremiah, and my husband, Steve, who are so wonderful about eating spaghetti or leftovers when I'm at the computer.

Chapter One

The shrill cries woke him.

Multimillionaire bachelor Max Stevens rolled over in bed and listened.

It couldn't be the television since his twin brother, Rand, and Rand's new wife, Elizabeth, were on an extended honeymoon. Besides, the sound of the TV wouldn't reach his suite of rooms.

None of the staff at the house he shared with his brother would dare turn on a TV while on duty. And gauging from the sky's pale light it was probably about 6:00 a.m.

Cats, he decided. Despite the gardener's attempts, strays had obviously gotten onto the grounds again and were fighting. Max pushed himself up in bed, the silk sheet sliding down his chest and pooling at his waist. It looked as if he would have to break up the fight himself since he could still hear the noise down on the patio.

Swinging his bare legs over the edge of the bed, his toes sank into the lush tan carpet. He slid his feet into slippers and grabbed his silk robe, shrugging it on over his paisley shorts. He doubted anyone was up yet. However, in a house this size, he could never be certain of not running into the staff. It was safer to stay decently covered.

As he walked to the balcony, he rubbed a weary hand over his face. This was not how he liked to be awakened early in the morning. He had a hard day of work ahead of him. Stevens Inc. was planning two more store openings across the country and with Rand gone, all the extra work fell to Max. Not that he begrudged Rand his vacation for a moment. Rand had been in a tailspin after losing his wife, Carolyn, almost two years ago. Blind and bitter, it had taken his occupational therapist, Elizabeth, who was now Rand's wife, to lead him back to the living. Eventually, Rand's sight improved and he began working at the office. Max had been grateful for Rand's help again. He wholeheartedly approved of his brother's extended honeymoon before coming back to work full-time. Max had held down the fort for over a year, what difference did a few extra months make?

Still, it would've been nice to have been done with his morning devotions and prayer *before* this interruption. His whole day would feel off-kilter now.

Padding down the balcony stairs, Max followed the wrought-iron railing around the curve to the patio below. But when he turned the corner, he stopped and stared in stunned amazement.

"Sarah!" It was his housekeeper's fault. It had to be. "Sarah, where are you!"

He continued to stare, rooted to the spot until he heard hurried footsteps. "Oh, mercy," the housekeeper said.

Her gasp told him he'd been wrong. "Do you have grandkids?"

"Certainly not. You know my husband and I wouldn't keep that a secret." She stood by him and stared too.

"Well, do something," he finally said.

"Like what?" she asked.

"You're a woman. Don't you know what to do about these things?"

"That's a sexist remark, Mr. Stevens."

Realizing she didn't intend to move from her position as an observer, he stepped forward. The sounds stopped. He raised an eyebrow as he peered into the laundry basket that contained the two toddlers.

"Well?" Sarah prodded.

He shot her a look that told her to mind her tongue and took another step forward. "They're sorta small, aren't they?"

"I guess. But you would know better than me."

He glanced over his shoulder. "And what do you mean by *that?*"

Sarah had been with the household since Max was five so Max's scowl didn't faze her in the least. Plopping her hands on her ample hips, she replied, "What do you think I mean? They look just like…look, there's a note."

Max plucked the piece of paper off the side of the laundry basket and began to read:

Dear Max,

I had no one else to leave them with. I'm in trouble, and have to leave. I know you'll take care of them and love them for me. Please don't tell anyone the secret. I've always thought they looked

like my knight in shining armor. I've never forgotten you. Thank you. You're a kind man.
P.S. Meet Maxwell Robert and Madeline Renée.

Max stared in disbelief at the note until a gurgle
from the basket drew his attention.

Maxwell and Madeline?

Two cherubic faces stared back at him. He wasn't
sure how old they were but he knew they were too big
to be newborns. And the writer of the note was right.
They did look like him. They both had dark hair and
one had deep brown eyes, hinting at a Cajun lineage.

But his?

Impossible! He knew that for certain. He wasn't promiscuous.

"Well, Mr. Stevens," Sarah said, her voice reeking
with disapproval. "Are you just going to leave your
kids here on the porch or bring them into the house?"
She pivoted and marched away before he could answer.

His kids.

Dear Father, he thought, staring at the two children
who were beginning to squirm against the bonds that
held the backs of their overalls to the handles of the
basket. *I know these aren't my kids. I know it. So,
would You mind telling me what I'm getting myself into
this time?*

God didn't answer.

Max took that to mean he would find out in time.
Inching forward, not sure if his nearness would set the
kids off, he picked up the two bulky blue-striped bags
that sat nearby and the laundry basket that held the two
tiny children.

The one with the brown eyes, he thought it was the

girl since it had a pink ribbon in its hair, gurgled and kicked its feet.

The other one chewed on its toe and studied Max with a serious expression.

"Well, uh, kids, I don't quite understand this, but for some reason your mommy left you with me. She sounded scared in the note. But don't worry. Hopefully, she'll be back soon because…to be honest, I don't have the faintest idea what to do with you. But maybe we can get along fine until…until we get this all worked out."

The blue-eyed child frowned and released his foot, kicking Max in the nose.

Max froze, afraid they'd start crying again.

The child wiggled his toes against Max's mouth as if offering him a taste.

Max grimaced and started to move slowly toward the door, deciding the kids would be better off on the floor inside, instead of trying to jam their feet down his throat.

Madeline laughed, which caused the other child to gurgle, too.

Relieved that they weren't going to throw a fit at his movements, Max hurried to the door. "I'm just going to take you inside now, and sit you down. I bet you're hungry. I am."

He paused at the doors leading into the study that overlooked the balcony. Fumbling, he managed to get the door open and make it inside. "I'm not sure exactly what you eat."

Suddenly, he sniffed, his nose wrinkling as his eyes narrowed suspiciously. "You're still in diapers, aren't you?" Kicking the door closed, he juggled the basket for a firmer grip.

"We're going to have to do something about that right now," he said, though he wasn't sure what. Smiling in relief at the accomplishment of getting them into the house without another bout of crying, he decided maybe this baby stuff wasn't going to be so bad—except for the odor emanating from one of them.

Setting the basket down by the sofa, he hollered, "Sarah!"

Both children immediately jumped, then burst into tears. The terror any bachelor immediately feels at the sight of such small children had been held at bay—until those shrieks. His eyes widened and he reached out and patted first one, then the other's shoulder. Yes, there was no doubt about it, he was in way over his head. He needed help.

"Sarah! Find me the employment agency's number."

Kaitland Summerville ran a hand wearily through the straight strands of her honey blond hair, pushing it back from her face. The action did no good, the blunt cut allowed it to fall right back against her smarting jaw.

Adjusting the ice pack, she tried to shuffle the paperwork that she was currently working on, but to no avail.

"Why don't you take a break?" her assistant, Shirley, asked, her lips quirking in exasperation. "If I'd just been through what you'd been through, I would. I still can't believe you've been temporarily pulled from working with the kids—"

Kaitland smiled, a weary smile. "I don't blame Jake one bit, Shirley. True, I did nothing to provoke Johnnie's daddy. He was drunk. But he and his wife are separated, and he doesn't have custody. And what happened *was* very traumatic for the kids. It's only natural that I step back until everything is settled. At least for the sake of the other kids and their parents. I wouldn't want to stay and risk any censure falling on the day care or the church.''

Kaitland set the ice pack down on the table and pulled out a compact to examine the swelling.

Today had started out a rotten day and had gone downhill from there. First thing this morning, her step-brother, Robert had called, trying to get her to go to a society function with him. She smiled wryly thinking of their conversation. She rarely went anywhere like that anymore. Still, he knew she did her best to have a forgiving nature and he was always wheedling, trying to get her to do things for him whenever he needed help. Sometimes she thought she'd rather be bitten by a rattler than to again circulate at the society events he frequented. These outings always ended in disaster. It was simply that he wasn't a Christian. They had nothing in common except their parents had married each other when Kaitland was a preteen. When she'd managed to avoid a commitment to attending the function with her stepbrother, she had thought things were looking up.

However, she'd gone out to her car, running late, only to find it wouldn't start. Just her luck. The water pump had been on its last legs for at least six months and she didn't have the money to pay for a new one. True, she was the director of the local day care in the small town of Zachary, Louisiana, but that wasn't always enough to make ends meet.

Disgusted, she'd called a cab, then a mechanic, hoping she could work out some sort of payment plan with him. The mechanic had agreed. But unfortunately for her, George had been driving the cab. George was the slowest driver in the world, she was sure of it. How he'd kept his license she didn't know. The ten-minute trip to work had taken twenty minutes.

Because of that she had been running even later. The chapel service they held for the older kids was therefore late starting, which threw everything else behind. And right into the middle of that had come Johnnie's daddy while she was outside; the daddy that had skipped out of town two months ago and left his wife and child destitute. He wanted his boy, as he'd said. She couldn't allow him to take the child and had sent Shirley to call the police.

That's when she'd been injured. Oh, she didn't think Johnnie's daddy had meant to hurt her. He'd only meant to move her aside so he could get to his boy. As far as she knew, Johnnie's father had never been of a violent nature. However, he'd pushed her and in the process he had tripped over one of those stupid shrubs that all businesses put out to look nice but only ended up getting in the way.

Trying to stop their fall by counterbalancing, Kaitland had shoved back against him, but the maneuver hadn't worked. She'd ended up with a table on top of her and he'd ended up going through a plate-glass window.

And some of the children had witnessed the scene.

The man was now at the hospital getting stitches—and sobering up—and she was sitting in the office nursing a bruised jaw.

And a temporary removal from the eyes of the parents and kids until her battered face healed. Instead of overseeing the day care for the rest of the week, her pastor, Jake, had suggested she stick with the paperwork until everything blew over. There had already been two calls from concerned parents—boy, did news travel fast in a small town. Since there was a board meeting scheduled in a few weeks, the pastor suggested they discuss the incident then. But he didn't expect any trouble. By then any worries would be gone, Jake had assured her, and she would be able to go back to work with no problems. But she still had to wait that long.

It couldn't get any worse.

Of course, looking at her jaw now, Kaitland saw only a very faint coloring to it. She didn't bruise easily. She knew that from five years ago....

Her eyes still held a slightly dull glaze, no doubt from the pain in her jaw.

"Well, at least you're not losing any pay while you're working in here with me, though you're probably going to be bored to death."

Kaitland smiled at Shirley, knowing she was right. Shirley was short, no more than five foot and had bright red hair and green eyes, fitting her Irish heritage. She also possessed the energy of ten people, one of the reasons Kaitland was so glad to hire her in the first place. Kaitland hated the paperwork and was glad when the day-care center had been able to afford a full-time bookkeeper/secretary, taking the burden off Kaitland's shoulders. Since Kaitland had helped found the day care, she'd done all the extra work. She could honestly say it was nice to be the director. Now she worked overseeing so much of what she hadn't particularly loved to do before. The only thing she really missed was working with the kids on a one-to-one basis.

"You're right," Kaitland told Shirley. "I'll be bored to death. I'd go ahead and take vacation right now, but I don't want Jake to think I'm bailing out on him."

"How about another job then?" a voice said.

Both women gasped. Kaitland's eyes shot to Jake, who'd just entered the room, afraid to believe what she'd just heard. As if realizing his mistake, he said, "I didn't mean that the way it sounded. I had a call from a friend who runs an employment agency. We have a mutual friend in need of a temporary nanny... Why don't you come into my office?"

Temporary nanny? She shot Shirley an odd look and followed the pastor into his office. Once they were seated, he continued, "I didn't mean to blurt that out. Sometimes my humor falls flat."

Jake Mathison was thirty-two, single, but also single-minded in his dedication to his job. He'd been enthusiastic four years ago when Kaitland had approached him about the idea of opening a day-care center in their church. He'd supported her every step of the way. So, Kaitland knew he didn't mean anything by what he'd said, but was curious anyway about what he'd meant. She sat patiently and waited as he rubbed one hand over his face.

"This is confidential." Jake leaned forward in the chair, his gaze meeting hers and showing her the seriousness of his statement. "That's why I brought you in here. This is something I *don't* want overheard by anyone." Placing his hands on the desk, he allowed a small smile to ease Kaitland. "As I said, a friend called the employment agency, needing a nanny. The person requires immediate help at his house. It seems that some kids were abandoned on his doorstep."

Kaitland's mouth dropped open. "Has he called Child Services?"

"No. No, there was a note. Um, well, the note intimated that the kids were his, though he denies it. He wants to find out what's going on before he does anything with the children. And the first thing he needs is a nanny.''

"Why me?"

"He didn't ask for you. He just asked the agency for someone who's not gossipy. I've known you for five years now, Kaitland," he said, calling her by the name everyone at church called her by. "I've never heard a word of gossip out of you. I feel I can trust you." He leaned slightly forward again, and with earnest eyes, added, "I also know you can use the extra money. Not only can you take your paid vacation if you want, but you'll be getting a salary, almost double what you're earning now, while you're on the job there."

"Double?" Kaitland gaped. She could sure use the money. Her grandmother's medical bills over the last year and a half, and then her funeral, had put Kaitland in debt. She was barely managing each month, which was ironic, considering her stepbrother was rich. But he'd refused to help their grandmother after she had disowned him. So, it was left to Kaitland to see to her grandmother's bills now that she was gone. And the taxes were past due on the house her grandmother had left her. She hated the thought of losing the place. Yet, now she was being given a possible solution to her dilemma. "Why is he willing to pay so much?" Then another thought crossed her mind. "Just who is he?"

"Discretion is part of his need. And he'd want you to live in. As for who he is…"

Jake leaned back and folded his hands across his flat stomach. Why did that gesture make her feel so uneasy?

"It's been a long five years for you, Kaitland."

Kaitland knew he was talking about the *incident,* as she thought of it.

"I've watched you recover from the circumstances, pull your life back together and conquer almost all of your fears. You're a strong woman, willing to work hard at the work God has called you to. Not only that, but you're devoted in your personal life, too. Sometimes we don't understand the trials we go through, but we have to remember that God lets us go through things to mold us how He wants us, into His image."

"What are you getting at, Jake?" Nervously, she gripped her damp palms together in her lap. She didn't like talking about that time. She had overcome most of what had happened.

That was the catch, though.

Most.

She knew there was still some bitterness and hurt there, but was at a loss how to let go of it.

"Getting on with your life, Kaitland," the pastor said. "I would never suggest anything that might hurt you. I feel you're ready for this." He paused, then, "The man is rich. I know your ex-fiancé was rich, too. I thought this might be the perfect opportunity for you to get out around that social set again and see that not all of them are like your ex-fiancé. Since I know this family and would trust them with my own sister, I feel you'd be safe. What do you say?"

Perspiration broke out on Kaitland's skin. She'd never told her pastor the name of her ex-fiancé as she'd started at this church after that fiasco. But her pastor talked about his friends a lot. It couldn't be…it just couldn't be.

Still, she so desperately needed the money, she knew

before she asked the next question that she was going to take the job. "Who is it?"

"You've heard me talk about Rand and Max Stevens?" he asked easily.

Her stomach sank to her toes even as she said, "I believe I have."

"Well, it seems there's been some sort of mix-up and Max Stevens needs you out there immediately."

Kaitland smiled. Max Stevens might need someone immediately, but she doubted he was going to appreciate seeing the woman he had jilted five years ago.

Nope, he wasn't going to want to see Kaitland at all.

But her pastor was right. Though he didn't realize it, he was giving her the perfect opportunity to lay her past to rest. Kaitland took a deep breath. She was going back into the lion's den and would come out unscathed this time.

Chapter Two

"Come here, che'rie. Just give me the baby powder and we'll be okay."

Max Stevens, covered from head to toe in white dust, was down on all fours near the edge of the queen-size bed, holding out his hand coaxingly as he peppered his speech with Cajun words, trying to persuade the diaper clad little girl to hand over the dusting powder.

Kaitland stood at the door and held back her laugh.

"*No!* No! No! No! No!" The toddler accentuated each no with a bounce of her knees and a squeeze of the powder container, which puffed out its fine white sheen all over the forest green carpet.

Max winced, shook his dark glossy hair in exasperation then promptly sneezed when he inhaled the dusty powder that floated in the air. Only a few hours had passed since he'd discovered the children, yet somehow, it felt longer. *Much* longer, Max reflected.

"Come on, che'rie. Just give it to Uncle Max and let me change your diaper."

"No!" the little girl squealed, then threw the container at him and turned, dancing away on her toes toward the bed.

"Thank you," he said with the desperation of one totally besieged, but saw relief in sight when the little girl started to crawl up on the bed. He placed his hand on the mauve and green comforter to push himself up, but the other twin, who had been trying to pull off his shirt, suddenly decided it was playtime.

"Horsey!" the young boy whooped. With a lunge, he shot forward, landing in the middle of Max's back.

"Oooaf!"

Max went down.

Kaitland burst into peels of laughter. "Felled by your own son, Max. I'm surprised. And you, who used to play football."

Max's head jerked around at the familiar voice and his eyes widened incredulously. "Katie?" he gasped.

"That's right, Max. At least you remember my name…or should I say the name *you've* always called me."

She strode into the room, gliding into it as if she had every right to be there. Ignoring him, she crossed to where the little girl was lying on the bed, one toe in her mouth, the other foot waving around as she waited for a diaper. Grabbing a diaper bag, Kaitland pulled out the wipes and then quickly, efficiently cleaned and diapered the child.

Max couldn't get over how good Katie looked as he knelt there in the middle of the powder-caked floor.

It had been five years. She hadn't aged, just gotten more graceful. Her honey blond hair was now straight instead of permed, but it was more beautiful, swaying to and fro with every step she took. She'd filled out a little, was more rounded, softer-looking, not as coltish as he remembered. Long, graceful hands worked quickly and expertly to diaper and dress the girl in a pink romper that was in the bag she'd pulled up onto the bed.

Her high cheekbones were slightly flushed with color and her lips were puckered as she made cooing noises to Maddie. Maddie laughed and kicked both feet in approval to whatever Kaitland had said.

And those eyes.

Her green eyes still sparkled like jewels when she laughed.

Five years and he'd thought never to see her in his house again... His eyes widened. "What are you doing here?" he blurted out, realizing he was seeing her in his house and had no idea why.

Kaitland glanced over her shoulder, a sardonic brow lifted. "I'm changing a diaper, Max. Don't tell me you've never seen a diaper changed."

Chagrined by her answer, Max opened his mouth to tell her he knew exactly what she was doing and that was not what he'd meant, but Kaitland continued, "The girl doesn't look much like you, but now the boy... My, Max, he could be your twin, but you already have one of those, don't you?" Her light tone was in contrast to her sudden intense stare at the child.

"They're not mine."

"Oh, really?" Kaitland asked, lifting Maddie in her arms. "And what is this one's name?" she asked, bouncing the little girl on her hip.

"Madeline Renée."

"And the boy?"

"Maxwell Robert," he replied, suddenly realizing how Kaitland would take the fact that the boy's first name was the same as his own.

"And he's not yours," she said so falsely that Max flushed. She was always able to goad his temper.

"No. *They are not!*" He enunciated each word.

"I see, little Max," she said, winking at the boy.

"I've been calling him Bobby."

"Bobby?" Kaitland asked before giving Maddie a peck and letting her down on the floor.

"Well, it would seem rather odd to call him Max, now, wouldn't it?" Max demanded as she crossed the room.

"I don't know," Kaitland mused aloud, pausing to tap her chin as if in deep thought. Then, for the first time, she pierced him with those deep green eyes. "A lot of people name their firstborn son after themselves."

"He's not my firstborn son!"

"You have another?" she asked, all innocence.

"I don't have any son," he growled, then took a deep breath. "Look. It's hard to explain. I woke up to what I thought was a cat brawl and found these two at the bottom of the balcony steps near the kitchen."

"I see."

"No. You don't see. I have no idea who they belong to. Though it's probably someone who reads those stupid rag magazines and believes I'm out to populate half of Louisiana."

"You sure it's not the other half that believes you're Mr. Perfect?"

He frowned at her words.

"I'm sorry, it was only a guess."

"I don't know," he finally said, brushing off his pants. "It doesn't really matter. All I can figure out is some woman dropped off her kids hoping I'd give them a better life. For all I know, Max and Maddie aren't their real names.''

Both children turned at those words. Kaitland laughed. "I'd say that's their correct names, all right. Now, as to their parentage—"

"They're not mine!" he said so forcefully that Kaitland's eyes widened.

"I wasn't going to say that."

"You've already said it twice."

"No. I said the boy looks like you." She smiled. "But if the shoe fits—"

"Things aren't always as they look," he muttered.

Kaitland suddenly lost her smile and even paled slightly. "Don't I know that," she murmured, the air in the room suddenly charged with memories, a time when things hadn't been like what they'd looked.

Max remembered that time with clarity, and remembered the irrefutable proof that he'd produced to show her he knew she had been lying to him. Pain that he thought long dead and buried resurfaced, grabbing his heart and giving it an unexpected squeeze. Longing swept through him. *If it could only have been different. If you hadn't lied to me, had even just trusted me a little.* But that was in the past, the best place for it to remain. These children were the present. *And* Katie's presence in his house.

Kaitland walked over to the door where he only now realized Sarah stood. "Someone needs to sweep up here, Sarah," Kaitland said. "Will you see to it?"

"Of course," his housekeeper replied, and with an infinitesimal nod turned crisply on her heel and strode off down the hall.

"Thank you," Kaitland called out and then returned

her attention to the room as she surveyed it through narrowed eyes.

"Wait a minute," Max protested as Kaitland looked around as if the room were a bug under a microscope. "You can't go ordering my servants around."

Max stepped away from the bed, attempting to disengage Bobby from where the child hung on to his pant legs. Looking down, he realized the child had drooled all over his trousers. "Aw, no," he moaned. "These are two-hundred-dollar slacks."

Grimacing, he pulled the child away and then, not knowing what to do, he lifted the boy into his arms.

"Have they had lunch?" Kaitland asked as she went around the room, picking up objects on lower tables and moving them to higher places and rearranging other things.

Max stared in disbelief, unable to figure out just what she thought she was doing. The baby suddenly grabbed Max's paisley tie and jerked. He tried to disengage the choke hold Bobby had on him. Looking distracted, he glanced away from the deceivingly cherubic bundle in his arms. "What?" he asked, already forgetting what Kaitland had said.

"Lunch, Max? Have you fed the children yet?" Kaitland looked downright exasperated with him. "I don't remember you having a memory or hearing problem. Has that changed lately?"

Max growled low in his throat, managed to disengage the child's unnaturally strong grip then snapped rather curtly, "No, Katie. That hasn't changed. I'm a little overwhelmed at the moment. I've never been around kids before, and never two at once... Watch out!"

He went running across the room to where Maddie

had just grabbed a tablecloth and pulled. Potpourri spilled everywhere. "No, no, Maddie, che'rie," he said. "Don't put that in your mouth."

Kaitland strolled over and picked up the cute little girl, easily removing the dried rose petals from the child's mouth. "This room is definitely not meant for children. Where are you keeping them?"

"Um…" He looked around the room, then shrugged sheepishly.

"Oh, Max. They can't stay in here. They need baby beds, and there are no child protectors in the plugs—"

"Child protectors?" He looked thoroughly confused.

"And those lamps won't last an hour. Kids tend to gravitate toward the forbidden. You need to get your staff up here and have them baby-proof this room right now. Get rid of all these tablecloths that hang down and replace them with shorter ones. The kids look to be about fifteen months, is that right?" Kaitland stared at him expectantly.

"I don't know." He felt like a helpless green recruit in an army full of generals—or one general in particular, he thought sourly, eyeing Kaitland with a suddenly wary eye.

She shot him a reproachful look, and he had the vague thought that she was thoroughly enjoying his discomfiture. This was the first time cool, debonair Max had ever been less than the perfect sophisticate in front of her.

"Well, that's about the right age," she continued. "They can walk, but still use things to pull themselves up."

Bobby began to fuss and Max looked panicked.

"Bounce him gently on your hip, like this," Kaitland instructed.

Max watched Katie bounce Maddie, then imitated her.

Bobby immediately threw up. "Ugh!" Max hollered and thrust the child out at arm's length.

"What did you feed them for lunch?" Kaitland demanded, instantly setting down Maddie and gathering Bobby to her.

Max looked at the brown stain with revulsion. "Cookies."

"And?" she asked when he didn't say anything else.

"And milk." What did she want? A whole list down to the bug Maddie had tried to eat from the floor the last time she'd gotten out of the chair that he'd had to sit her in every two minutes.

"That's all?" Kaitland's eyes widened.

"They seemed to like it," he added defensively, realizing belatedly that his mother had never allowed him cookies for any meal when he had been a child...or, come to think of it, as an adult, before she'd died.

"They'll both have tummyaches," she warned.

As if out of sympathy with her brother, Maddie suddenly tossed her own cookies, all over the green carpet. Kaitland gathered her up in her free arm. "There there, little one," she comforted as the baby began to whimper.

"Well, this room is definitely out for a while. Find me a nearly empty room for these two...maybe your library, and bring some blankets. It's nap time. I need to put them down and then we'll talk."

"Talk? About what?"

"Why, their schedule. What else?"

"Their schedule? You make them sound like army recruits."

"You really don't know anything about babies, do you?"

Max ran a weary hand through his hair. "You know I don't. But I've sent for someone from the agency. I was assured they'd have someone out here by this afternoon."

Max's eyes suddenly narrowed. "Which brings me back to the original question I was going to ask you before you sidetracked me. What are you doing here?"

"Surprise," Kaitland said brightly and headed toward the door.

"Surprise? What does that mean?" he asked, grabbing the diaper bags and starting after her.

"It means, Max, that I'm the new nanny."

The thud of the bags hitting the floor could be heard all the way out in the hall.

Chapter Three

"No! No way! You're not staying."

Kaitland winced at Max's adamant tone. However, that didn't stop her from heading down the stairs. She refused to stand there and argue, with two sleepy kids in her arms.

"Katie, are you listening to me? I said no way!"

"I'm not deaf, nor do I even pretend to be," she replied, entering the library. "Oh, my, have you changed this into an office?" Papers covered the tops of two desks and new equipment had been added.

"Rand and I do a lot of day-to-day work here. I tend to go into the office only two or three times a week."

Ignoring him, she went to the plush tan sofa. Setting the children down on their feet, she quickly pulled the throw blanket off the back—this used to be Max's favorite spot to relax when she'd known him, and he always kept a blanket there—and spread it over the leather. Picking the children up, she lay them down one by one and tucked the blanket around them.

"No!" Maddie yelled, then immediately stuffed two fingers in her mouth, closing her eyes.

Bobby whined, then, grabbing the blanket, he curled it against his cheek and with a shuddering sigh was out.

"They were exhausted," Max whispered, stunned, absently handing Kaitland the blanket he'd grabbed on his way out the bedroom door.

"I imagine they've had a full day and night," Kaitland murmured softly, putting the blanket and some throw pillows as padding on the floor next to the sofa in case one of them accidently fell off.

She heard Max inhale and knew he was about to blast her. "Shh," she said, and motioned toward the door.

Max nodded curtly and went into the hall. With the door pulled almost closed, she turned to him. "It's been a long time, Max."

Looking disconcerted, Max stared for a moment then sighed. "Yeah, Katie, it has. Long enough that I had decided I'd never see you again."

He started toward a small sitting room where the family gathered at night to watch TV.

"Surely you knew someday we'd see each other again, Max?"

"I hadn't expected it under these circumstances," he muttered.

Kaitland laughed. "You were expecting these circumstances?"

"Of course not," Max said curtly, then apologized. "I'm sorry for snapping. But you could have given me a warning you were coming."

"What would you have said if I'd called and told you it was me the agency hired?"

He scowled.

"That's what I thought."

"Surely you don't want to work for me, do you?"

Kaitland's smile turned wistful. *I'd like a lot more,* she thought. "What do you think?"

Inside the cozy room he went straight to the phone and dialed the agency.

"Max, wait," she pleaded.

His gaze turned tortured for only an instant before hardening. "Yes, this is Max Stevens," he said to the person on the other end of the phone. "When I called this morning, I asked for an older woman, Christian, fifty or so, the grandmotherly type." He paused. "I see." There was another pause. "There's *no one* else?" Casting a harassed look at Kaitland, he replied, "Thank you."

Kaitland stared at Max, waiting for the ax to fall. When he didn't speak, she took hope and pleaded her case. "It's not going to be that bad, Max. The kids won't be any trouble. And as you've said, you don't know the first thing about them. Besides, I'm an emergency foster parent. I'm used to dealing with kids in stressful situations."

"What happened to your job at the day-care center?"

"You know about that?" She had been his secretary years ago, before the incident, but hadn't realized he knew anything about her life after they'd broken up.

He shrugged. "Jake talks about his church."

"I still work there. I'm on a leave of absence."

"What happened? Why?"

It was her turn to shrug. "I had an accident with a belligerent parent. My pastor thought it best to keep me out of the spotlight. Especially if my cheek bruises.''

Max's gaze sharpened and he came forward. ''You were hit?'' he demanded, taking her face in his hands and tilting it toward the east window.

His hands felt good. His touch awoke old memories in her, memories of when he'd held her tenderly within his embrace and kissed her good-night, leaving her with his own reluctance to part for even so short a time. Longing, deep and painful, filled her chest. His scent was still the same, spicy, musky. *Oh, Father, how can I stand this?* she silently asked.

Max's thumb ran over the slight swelling that her hair almost concealed. His breath fanned her face as his thumb stroked back and forth. Suddenly, realizing what he was doing, he released her and stepped back.

''I wasn't hit,'' she replied, just a little husky, despite her accelerated heart rate. ''A table fell on me when the man and I tripped.''

He said nothing for a moment, then, ''I don't see how this can work, Katie. There's just too much past between us.''

Panicked, she decided to play her trump card. Max was a good man despite his unwillingness to forgive her so many years ago and his determination in suspecting her of lying. She didn't want to tell him this, but seeing him now, she realized there was something still between them, something that had to be settled one way or another. And if he wasn't willing to make the effort, she suddenly was.

''I need the job, Max. If I can't get a new one within the month...'' she paused. Should she tell Max she'd lose her house? No, she decided, it seemed too much like begging. She had some pride, after all. "I'll have some serious problems," she concluded.

Max whipped around to stare at her. "But why? Your stepbrother—"

"Refuses to help me," she replied before he could remind her how rich her stepbrother was.

That was a sore point she'd not quite gotten over in reference to her grandmother's health. Her grandmother had disowned Robert just before she fell ill with cancer. Kaitland was never sure why. Her grandmother never told her the cause of it. Somehow her grandmother had her will changed without Kaitland knowing it. When it was read, Kaitland was stunned to find out the house and almost all of the money that was left belonged to her. What little money there was ran out before the hospital bills and funeral were paid for.

"If you need money—" Max said, interrupting her thoughts.

"Don't even say it," Kaitland warned, her eyes narrowing. "After what *has* gone on between us, it would be wrong if you offered me anything."

"But you'll *work* for me."

Kaitland flushed just a little. "Yes."

She knew it didn't make sense to Max. They had almost married, which should have made her more amenable to accepting a loan, but for her it was just the opposite. No, it would be easier to work for him and not feel indebted.

"You aren't making this easy for me, Katie," he finally said, running a weary hand through his hair.

"I hope not," she replied brightly, despite the tension.

He shot her an exasperated look. "Fine. You have the job. But, before you celebrate, I want to lay down some ground rules. The past is the past. We leave it there. This is strictly an employer-employee relationship. Your job is to take care of the children, see they are cared for and want for nothing. You only need to tell me what to get and it'll be done. Is that understood?''

"Yes, Max."

"Well, good."

She hid her smile. Max looked as if he thought he'd lost the battle but couldn't figure out why. She knew why. Just by being in the same house, the past was going to creep up until it was dealt with and taken care of.

"First we'll need cribs for the children. With that they'll need sheets and bumper pads and a couple of light blankets. What about some clothes? Do you want me to run over to the church and check their clothes closet—''

"I can certainly buy anything the children need," Max replied, affronted.

Kaitland paused, then asked the question that had been burning in her since she'd first arrived. She'd known the kids weren't Max's. He lived by the moral code of his faith. She took his word, too, for Max also didn't lie. "Why do you insist on seeing to this problem? You could call Child Services and the children would be taken away and you'd never have to be responsible for them again."

"But I am responsible."

Her eyes widened in shock, thinking she had misjudged him.

"Not that way," he replied, clearly exasperated. He dropped wearily onto the couch. Leaning his head back, he closed his eyes. "Someone left them on my patio with a note addressed to me. I don't know if the person was a crackpot or someone who really thought I could help the children. But whoever it was put their trust and faith in me. I won't palm that off on some overworked agency that would probably separate the children out of necessity.''

Kaitland nodded. That would probably happen. Though Child Services didn't like to do that, they had to find somewhere for the children.

"I have plenty of money," he said. "Enough to last two lifetimes. And this house is big enough to hold forty or fifty people. So there's plenty of room. It won't hurt to keep them here.''

She smiled, gently, doing her best to hide the misting of her eyes. "You're a good person, Max Stevens.''

"No, just practical," he argued gruffly, refusing praise as he always did. "I'm going to call one of the investigative people we use in our business. I'll put him on the case and see if he can find out what happened to the mother. After all, how hard is it going to be to track down a set of twins that were born about…fifteen months?'' At her nod, he continued, "About fifteen months ago.''

"I honestly don't know. I imagine easier than tracking down a single child.''

"My thoughts exactly. So, I figure within a week, maybe two, we'll have this all cleared up.''

She hoped they had more than just that cleared up, but she didn't say so. "Are you going to order the cribs and clothes, or do you want me to go shopping. I should warn you, if I go shopping, the children will be left here with you.''

His eyes widened. "I'll call my store immediately. It's nice owning a large chain of retail stores.'' He suddenly grinned. "I'll have my secretary at the office go downstairs to the store and find someone who knows about babies and send over everything they'll need. *Two* of everything," he amended. "That should work."

Kaitland shook her head in disbelief.

"Now, about my office. When do I get it back?"

Kaitland shrugged. "I imagine when the kids wake up, which could be anywhere from an hour to two hours."

"But I've got a lot of work to do," he began.

"Bring it in here," she replied.

Grumbling, he stood and walked out of the room, listing to her or himself, she wasn't sure, what he needed to accomplish today.

Same old Max, except she didn't remember him taking quite this much interest in the business five years ago.

She headed up the stairs to the room where the children had been. She found the maid, Lavina, in there finishing cleaning up the mess. "You'll need to get someone up here to take all the knickknacks out of this room, Lavina. They'll also need to remove the bed. Mr. Stevens is turning it into a nursery for the twins."

"I'll get Tim from the stables to help me this afternoon," the maid said.

"You'd better go ahead and do it now," Kaitland told her. "Mr. Stevens is ordering cribs and I imagine they'll be here in an hour or two. Also, do you know which room I'm staying in?"

"Oh, I'm sorry, Miss Summerville. Sarah told me to put your bags in the room across the hall, unless you want the one across from Mr. Stevens?"

She knew Max's room was next door to the babies'

room. The one next to her would be across the hall from him and larger than the one she was in. "No. This is fine. I need to be close to the children. As a matter of fact, if you could find a small twin bed I might just sleep in here."

"Oh, no, ma'am. Sarah wouldn't approve of that at all. She was telling me how much she likes you and has missed you around here. She'd be very upset if you weren't completely comfortable while you were here."

Kaitland grinned. That sounded just like Sarah. "Very well. Thank you, Lavina."

"And Darlene is to help you with the babies whenever you need it. Sarah said those two are too much for one person. She said of course Mr. Stevens, being a bachelor, wouldn't know, nor would he remember how much of a handful he and his brother were. She said that he deserved a taste of what he'd put her through growing up. I think she's quite excited about having the little mites in the house."

Kaitland's grin turned into a full-blown smile. "I'm glad. You tell Sarah I'm sure Max is going to get a great big taste of what it's like to have two toddlers underfoot. Now, go on. I need to unpack."

She walked across the hall to her suite. Pushing open the door, she immediately smiled in pleasure. Light mauves and browns decorated the space. There were no balcony doors like the room across the hall, but the shutters on the large window made it possible for her to keep the room as bright as day or dimly lit. A large overstuffed, floral-print couch sat near two armchairs, creating a comfortable sitting area. A polished oak armoire held a TV and VCR, as well as a stereo. A low bookcase held a collection of interesting titles. She

knew the door to the right was the bedroom and bathroom.

Crossing the plush carpet, she found out she was
right. Max's room was larger. She knew he had a small
gym in the second room off the main room, as did
Rand. Max had explained the layout of the house once
to her.

"Oh, my," she breathed, looking in the room. Yel-
lows and green pastels decorated the bedroom, along
with pink and blue pastel watercolors hanging on the
walls. She wondered who had decorated this. Certainly
not an interior decorator. Her bag was sitting on the
bed. She unpacked, putting everything in the cherry-
wood armoire as she went. Her last thing to unpack
was the first thing she had packed—her Bible.

Taking it out, she sat down on the bed and opened
it. She was surprised to find she had opened it to a
familiar scripture, *"You will not fear,"* it started, and
ended with, *"I will be with him in trouble, I will deliver
him and honor him."*

Smoothing her hand over the worn pages, she
prayed, "Father, please help me, guide me in what You
would have me do. I thought this would be so easy,
coming here and facing the past. But, well, I've discovered I still have some kind of feelings for Max. Oh,
I'm not sure what they are, but they're there. I don't
want to hurt Max again, but I refuse to put myself in
the path of hurt, either. Open the doors for healing
between us even if that means we solve the problems
and never see each other again. All I know is this has
to come to a head. Thank You, Father."

She laid her Bible down and stood. Taking her suit-
case, she tucked it under the bed and then turned toward the door.

"Round one goes to Daniel," she whispered. She had faced the lion in his den and come out unscathed.

"Now let's see what happens in round two," she murmured.

Chapter Four

"I've got Dugan Lawrence, head of security at our
stores, checking into the twins' background," Max
said, hanging up the phone and turning to where Kaitland had just entered the den. "And Jennifer is buying
the store out, if I know her."

"Jennifer?" Kaitland asked quizzically.

"My secretary. She loves kids and became my secretary when Rand had his accident."

Max watched Kaitland digest that as she seated herself across from him in one of the overstuffed chairs.
He couldn't get over how good she looked. His heart
beat a staccato as he unobtrusively studied her again.
She was like manna for a starved soul. He thought he'd
gotten over her, was no longer empty without her, but
seeing her now... He forced himself to push those feelings aside and remember how she'd betrayed him. It
would not be good to act the fool again. "Do you have
any problems with living in? What about your own
house or your job?"

"Jake gave me time off. I'm on vacation. I have four

weeks built up but hadn't taken any of it until now. As for my house, I imagine if I can run by once or twice a week, it'll be okay. I can call and stop the paper, and my mail all goes to a post-office box anyway.'' She shrugged daintily. ''There's nothing else to worry about.''

''What about personal phone calls and such? Do you need to forward your phone?''

''No. The only people who would need to get in touch with me are at the church. Jake will forward any urgent messages to me.''

He nodded. ''About publicity. I'd like to keep this situation quiet. You know how the news media constantly hounds Rand and me. This would be a field day. Not that I have anything to hide. But I'd like to have some answers, know who these kids belong to before this hits the papers.''

''I understand.''

''But?'' he asked, seeing the look on her face.

She hesitated. ''I'd as soon not be in the middle of a media feeding frenzy, either. If you'll remember, I almost was, five years ago…''

''I thought we agreed to keep the past in the past?'' Max asked, his tone harsher than he'd intended.

Kaitland sighed. ''I'm sorry. You asked.''

''Yes, I did. And yeah, I wondered why those pictures never hit the newsstands.''

''Oh, Max, you had that all figured out. Remember, I was in on the conspiracy with whoever it was that slipped you the pictures. They were angry at me and wanted to make sure you knew I didn't really love you.''

''Katie,'' Max began.

''You brought this up, Max,'' Kaitland said, remembering those years when she had waited day after day then week after week until she had figured out that the sick person who had snapped pictures of her and ruined her soon-to-be marriage was not planning to release the photos to the media and ruin the rest of her life, as well.

"I don't want to fight," he warned.

"Oh, no, of course not," Kaitland said gently, defeat in her voice. "It was easier to accept what you saw in those pictures and find me guilty."

"You can't deny you were in Senator Richardson's arms kissing him," Max said desperately, the old pain boiling up anew. "I saw the pictures. How can you explain it?"

Kaitland smiled, but it wasn't a smile of pleasure. She remembered that night. Going up to her step-brother's room. She'd thought, at the time, that the note sent to her had been from her stepbrother. Who else would call her to his bedroom in the middle of a party? Of course, later she realized that the person had simply gotten their rooms mixed up. Her and her stepbrother had connecting rooms. But at the time, she had simply thought her brother might be ill.

She'd found out differently. Going into the darkened room, looking around, she had been surprised when large muscular hands had closed around her shoulders. Gasping, she had spun around, only to see Senator Richardson, very drunk, standing there smiling at her. She remembered his words about *inviting, her room* and *cook up our own little fun*. Realizing his intentions, she had backed away, but he'd thought it funny, some grand game. It was during that struggle that someone had snapped shots of their intimate embrace.

She almost shuddered, remembering how close she'd

come to getting raped. Shame had prodded her not to tell anyone of the fiasco in the bedroom. Since she was spending the night, she had escaped to her room and changed her ruined gown. But she'd not gone back down to the party. She'd hidden in her room, crying over what had almost happened.

And if she'd pulled away from Max's touch for the next few weeks it had only increased her shame, and her inability to explain why she suddenly didn't want to be touched.

She hadn't been able to tell him, certain he would look at her differently. When she'd finally decided to confess, it was too late. That someone else who had evidently witnessed her humiliation and taken pictures had sent them to Max. Yeah, she didn't much like the media, either, for whoever the scum was that had taken the pictures had certainly gotten revenge. She still couldn't understand why one of the magazines hadn't bought them…assuming that is what happened, as she was almost certain it was.

"That's the problem, isn't it?" she said sadly now. "You never once asked me to explain the pictures. You just waited until I showed up for our date that night and then dropped the pictures in my lap and told me they had been delivered to you, anonymously. And since they were pictures of the bash over a month before, the one you didn't go to with me, it was obvious, according to you, that I was not as committed to the relationship as you were."

"You never even offered an explanation," Max argued.

"You should have trusted me," Kaitland said unhappily.

"But the pictures..." Max raised his hands helplessly, then let them fall back to his sides.

Kaitland saw the hurt and pain that she was sure was mirrored on her own face. She remembered her terror when she'd seen the pictures, the sinking sensation in the pit of her stomach when Max had stared so coldly down at her. She had opened her mouth to explain, but suddenly realized all of her fears were coming true. Max was not going to believe whatever she said. She was doomed to even try. And belatedly, she realized the main reason he wouldn't believe her was because she had not been the one to tell him. Still, the pictures were so incriminating.

"Yet you won't explain?" he said now.

Pride stiffened Kaitland's spine. It would do no good. She knew his mind was set against her. Had those pictures not shown up, they would have worked through the situation, but all Max could see was that she had not come to him until someone else had implicated her so he believed what he saw in the photos. "No," she finally said, thinking it useless to argue further.

He shook his head. "Then it's best we forget it and remember this is only a job between us."

Kaitland's heart breaking, she nodded. "Agreed, again."

"Very well." Max cleared his throat and wiped the emotion from his face. Kaitland could still see what he thought of as her betrayal burning in his eyes. "I told Jennifer to have the furniture delivered by noon today. I'll be calling my lawyers to make sure we're not breaking any laws by keeping the kids here. Would you be willing to act as an emergency foster parent should the need arise?"

Kaitland inclined her head. "Of course. I imagine, though, you won't have any problem housing them here temporarily since the note was left for you."

"How do you know about the note?" he asked, surprised.

"Sarah showed it to me."

Max rolled his eyes. "I should have known."

Kaitland giggled, the tension between them finally easing. "She was ecstatic at the thought that you might be getting served back some of what you put her through when you were a child."

"Hey, it was Rand, not me, that drove the woman to gray prematurely."

"Not according to her," she replied. "You were, after all, the one with all the broken bones each time something went awry."

"But it was Rand who masterminded the situations."

"We only have your word for that," she said, smiling with the good memories they had once shared. "As I remember, Rand has a completely different story."

"Ask Elizabeth. I'm sure Rand has told her the truth."

"I know Elizabeth," Kaitland said. "And I'm sure she wouldn't divulge a secret Rand might share."

Max's smile immediately dimmed. Kaitland realized the issue of trust between Rand and Elizabeth had reminded Max of the betrayed trust he felt Kaitland had dealt him. "If you'll excuse me, Max. I need to get upstairs and make sure everything has been moved," she said abruptly. "I've got Darlene sitting with the little ones right now. She'll be helping me out as I need it. After making sure Sarah has a menu for the children, I'll go relieve Darlene. Bobby and Maddie should be awake by then and I'll take them outside to play until the room is ready. You'll have your office back and can work in peace."

Max nodded. "If they need anything, come tell me."

Kaitland imitated Max's nod, so formal, polite and distant. "I'll do that."

She stood and strode from the room.

Max sighed, his rigid posture deflating the minute Kaitland was out of sight. She'd just had to bring up those pictures. It seemed like only yesterday when a courier had hand-delivered the package to him. Thinking it was something Rand had sent over from the store, Max had strolled into his office/gym in his room upstairs. He was running late. Kaitland was due any minute and he still had his cuff links to apply and his jacket to slip into. He'd bought a special gift, a matching necklace to go with the ring he planned to give her tonight. Oh, they were engaged, but the ring she had worn was his mother's. He'd asked her to wear that until he found the perfect ring for her—which he'd discovered and which had just been delivered that day. A beautiful teardrop emerald surrounded with diamonds. The wedding band was emeralds with clusters of diamonds around them. It was exquisite. And to go with the ring was a matching necklace. He knew the color would bring out the glow of Kaitland's eyes, accentuate the gold highlights in her hair.

He could hardly wait to present it to her over dinner.

Grabbing his letter opener, he'd slit the manila envelope, tipping it so the papers would slide out.

Pictures had slid out instead. Pictures and a note demanding money.

Pictures of Kaitland and Senator Richardson as he kissed her, his arms wrapped around her, holding her tightly to him. A picture of Richardson falling onto the bed with her while her hands tangled in his jacket, her own leg showing up to her thigh. Another of the senator's hand pulling her dress from her shoulder while her head was flung back in abandon.

His face had flushed hot before every bit of blood had drained from it. He'd dropped into a chair, certain he was going to pass out. Then he'd thrown up.

His stomach had twisted with rage. He'd wanted to go out and destroy the senator with his bare hands. And Kaitland. He'd almost cried over the pain of her betrayal. He probably would have, had Sarah not chosen that moment to tell him Kaitland was there.

Instead, holding on to every shred of dignity he could muster, he'd marched downstairs and dropped the pictures in her lap, wanting her to break down and tell him they were a lie. Even though he *knew* they couldn't be, he wanted her to tell him that.

But when she'd paled and looked guiltily up at him, he'd known the truth. She was seeing the senator. All of her odd skittishness the past month suddenly made sense. And he'd thought it had been because he hadn't given her the official engagement ring yet. The joke had been on him. She hadn't wanted a ring, was probably flinching at the thought of having to wear it when she was interested in someone else.

He'd never felt such pain or betrayal as in that moment, especially when he accused her and she didn't deny it. No, she'd simply stood, with an unfathomable look in her eyes, and turned and walked out the door.

And he hadn't seen her since.

In five long years.

Except in his dreams. Yet those dreams were less

and less frequently, and through prayer he had been certain he had put her behind him.

Then she showed up on his doorstep, just when he was finally going forward again with his life. He'd found his niche at work, had plenty to keep him busy, had even been thinking about asking his secretary out, though he wasn't really interested in her romantically.

"Katie." He whispered her name out loud, shuddering at the feelings just saying her name evoked. "And I'm fool enough to keep you on, even when I realized what you're here for."

Well, what had he hoped her to be here for? To start up their relationship again? Preposterous. It was way too late for that. He should have known she was here for the kids, not to see him. But for one tiny moment he had forgotten everything. When she'd first walked through the door, he had remembered the feeling of joy, of contentment, before the ugly memories had rushed in.

"I was a fool," he repeated. "A total fool if I think I'm going to get any work done with you in this house."

Hearing his own weak voice, he vowed not to let Kaitland Summerville interrupt his life in the least. No, he *would* continue to work, *would* ignore her presence, *would* get on with his life as he'd been doing for the past five years. And she wasn't going to stop him.

Standing, he left the library, heading toward his office. She was not going to bother him in the least. Everything was going to proceed according to his neat little schedule, and peace would again reign in his house.

Chapter Five

"Sarah! Katie! Get in here!"

Peace, indeed, he thought sourly. Had it only been a half hour ago he had thought that? "Darlene, grab Maddie. No! Not the fax—"

The crash sounded all the way into the hall.

"I'm so sorry, Mr. Stevens. I thought they were asleep so I just ran to the bathroom…"

Max looked in dismay to the overturned fax machine. The beep of an incoming fax had obviously been the culprit behind the kids' untimely wakening. But the fax wasn't the only casualty. His desktop had been cleared and Bobby sat in the middle of it, eating a pencil.

Maddie was covered with dirt from the plant she had dug up, one of his Easter lilies or prayer plants or something. He wasn't sure of the name of the plant that opened only occasionally. The tan carpet was dotted with little footprints that reminded him of a bear cub. It looked as if one of the children—probably Maddie since he knew her propensity for dancing—had padded in little circles all over the floor.

Running to Bobby, Max immediately removed the pencil from the child's mouth, only to find a rubber band in his mouth, too, and... "Ouch!" He jerked his finger back, looking at the red swollen digit.

Bobby simply grinned toothily at him then spit out what looked like his eraser...or what was left of it. "Open up," Max said, wanting to check, but afraid to stick his finger back in there.

"Oh, no, Maddie. No. No!"

Max looked over at Darlene and groaned. The contracts his secretary had sent over were demolished. Even now Darlene was digging pieces of paper out of Maddie's mouth. Those that the little girl hadn't tried to eat were covered with muddy little paw prints.

"What happened?" Kaitland came running into the room, her eyes widening in despair at the signs of chaos. She hesitated, not sure which child to take until Max held Bobby up.

"I'm sorry. I didn't know they were awake. I was in with Sarah—" She stopped midsentence, looking at Max with growing dismay.

Max didn't have to ask why. He felt the warm liquid running down Bobby's leg wetting his tan shirt. "His diaper is leaking," Max said bleakly, thinking that at this rate his dry-cleaning bill was going to bankrupt his company.

"I'm sorry, Max," Kaitland said. "I'll just take him. Darlene, bring Maddie. I'll, uh, come back and clean up..."

"Let Darlene or Sarah see to that."

"Of course, Max."

She turned toward the door, talking to Bobby as she hurried out.

"And Katie?" Max called, picking up the ruined contracts and looking at the chew marks on them.

Kaitland paused, glancing warily back at Max. "Yes?"

"I think Maddie's hungry."

"Yes, Max," she said and scuttled out the door. Then to Sarah, "Could you get the children some carrot sticks. I'm going to take these two out back where they can wear off some of their energy."

Toting one child in each arm, Kaitland went into the library and grabbed the checked quilt then went out back. She avoided the formal gardens—no telling what they'd eat there—and the pool area. Instead, she went farther out toward the outer wall where there was a huge section of green lawn. The children could run there and do little damage.

"Here you go," Sarah called, huffing up behind Kaitland.

"Oh, thank you," Kaitland said, gratefully seeing not only the snacks, but drinks, a washcloth and a diaper bag, too.

She spread the blanket then called both children.

Maddie immediately came over and plopped down on the quilt. "It's going to take a little longer for little Bobby to get used to his nickname," Sarah said, bringing Maxwell Robert over to where Kaitland was. She dropped by her with a groan. "Should have gotten closer to a bench, young lady," Sarah grouched good-naturedly.

"I'm sorry, Sarah," Kaitland responded, even as she wiped up Maddie. She exchanged children with Sarah and went to work on Bobby, including changing the sopping-wet diaper.

She pulled out the snacks and sipper cups from the bag and said a quick prayer with the children. Amazingly, they both settled right down and began munching their snacks. "Good thing they like this. I wasn't sure what to fix them. I guess it's just going to take time for us to figure out what food they like."

"The way those two wolfed down the cookies Max fed them earlier, I doubt you're going to find very little those two don't like to eat."

Kaitland sighed as she watched the two little ones exchange snacks and resume eating. "They're so adorable," she said. "But at the rate everything has gone this morning, I'm afraid Max will let me go before I have a chance to find out their likes and dislikes."

"Oh, pshaw," Sarah said. "I have to disagree with you, Kaitland, dear. I haven't seen Max this animated in years. Not since you left his life."

"Since he dismissed me from it, you mean."

Sarah leaned forward and patted Kaitland's hand. "Don't know why you've waited so long to come back and straighten it out. Should have been taken care of a long time ago, if you ask me. But of course, Max is so closemouthed. It doesn't matter what happened back then. It's obvious Max still cares for you."

Kaitland raised surprised eyebrows. "What in the world makes you say that? It's obvious every time I'm in the room that Max is in a foul mood and can't wait to get away."

"Exactly."

Kaitland wrinkled her forehead in confusion. "You're not making sense."

"Of course I am. Ever heard the old saying, where there's a spark, you can get a fire going?"

Kaitland laughed. "Yeah, but don't you know an out-of-control fire can destroy everything around it?"

"Not this, dear. Max is led by God, and so are you. You're both just too stubborn to forgive and forget, though. When Max finally let's go of his hurt, I think you're gonna find that fire back. But with God tempering it, it ain't gonna get too out of control that either one of you gets hurt again, if you both remember to rely on God this time."

Kaitland blinked back sudden tears. *If they relied on God this time.* How true. When they'd had their problems before, instead of turning to God for help, they'd both allowed their wounded pride to stand in the way. That had caused untold problems. However, unlike Sarah, Kaitland didn't believe this was a second chance. She just wanted to make peace so she could get on with her life. She knew Max would never trust her again, not that she couldn't really blame him. Her mistake had cost her someone very dear to her. If she and Max could part as friends, she would take that and be happy. If Max could only forgive and forget. That was the key. And with her in the house, around him every day, that might happen.

"I hope you're right, Sarah. I'd like the pain between us healed."

"Ms. Summerville?"

Kaitland glanced up to where Darlene stood. "I wanted to let you know the furniture has arrived. I've got some people working on arranging the room right now. And there's someone here to see you."

"Me?" The only person Kaitland could think of was

Jake. "Could you stay with Bobby and Maddie?" she asked Darlene.

"Sure. I led the person to the gardens. I wasn't sure where to put him..."

"That's fine," Kaitland said, wondering where Timms, the butler, was.

"And I have to get back to cooking," Sarah said. "Don't you let them young 'uns outta your sight, Darlene. You hear me?" Sarah added, heaving her body up off the ground.

"Yes, ma'am," Darlene said, sitting down next to the children. Bobby immediately plopped into her arms. Maddie, obviously feeling left out, pushed her brother then squirmed up next to him on Darlene's lap.

Kaitland laughed and, with a kiss to each one's head, she turned and headed toward the gardens. Who in the world could it be that had come to visit her?

Then she spotted the dark brown head and knew.

Her stepbrother, Robert.

Robert and Max didn't get along. Darlene wouldn't want to leave him where Max might run into him. Kaitland had never understood the hostilities between the two men. She knew Max didn't approve of Robert's lifestyle, but he'd never discussed it with her, just told her to be careful around Robert. What could her stepbrother do to her that Max worried about—or had worried about, she amended.

Except take her to a party where she ended up getting attacked, she told herself. Well, Max had been right and she'd learned her lesson.

"Robert," she said, stopping at the garden gate where Robert stood. "What are you doing here?"

"I couldn't believe it when your pastor told me where to reach you," he said. In many ways, his dark brown eyes and dark complexion reminded her of Max. He, too, had Cajun blood in him from his mother's side of the family. Whereas Kaitland was light and fair, taking after her mother, Robert took after his mother. Her father, who was Irish, left only his green eyes and gold highlights to Kaitland.

Robert, being no blood relation, had no look of the family about him. Of course, her grandmother had raised them most of their life as their parents had died in a tragic car accident not long after they married. With no relatives, Robert had been raised by Kaitland's grandmother, too.

That was part of the ongoing tension between them now. Robert had never thought Kaitland's grandmother cared for him. And Kaitland refused to listen to Robert bad-mouth the woman who had raised them both. That was one reason she was so surprised to see him.

"Max Stevens needed a sitter. I was available."

"Those his kids?" Robert asked, nodding toward where the two little children sat playing with Darlene.

"No, those aren't his kids."

"Then what's he doing with them?"

Kaitland sighed. "Don't ask me to gossip about my boss, Robert. You know I won't do it. Suffice it to say, they aren't his children."

"Your boss, huh?" Robert asked.

"Yes, my boss."

"He was once much more."

"Robert," Kaitland warned. Robert was not a Christian, and scorned anything to do with church. He loved to find anything at all to needle Kaitland with when it came to morals.

"Okay, okay," Robert finally relented. "I don't know how you could work for the man after what he did, but that's up to you. I just wanted to check on you and find out what happened at the day care to send you running off.''

"I wasn't running off." Pushing open the gate, she headed down the curving pathway, ignoring the sweet fragrance of roses and azaleas, the climbing honeysuckle bushes, until she arrived at a bench. Seating herself, she motioned to Robert, who had followed her, then told him about the confrontation she'd had with the man at the day care. "Jake felt it was better for the children who witnessed the incident, and their parents, if I took some time off," she finished. "This job was available. So, after reassuring the children that there was no harm done, I came out here for the next few weeks. Besides, Jake has been encouraging me to relax. The pressure of the expansion project we're planning has been exhausting and he thought that coming here and straightening everything out might give me a chance to clear the air of the past. Satisfied?'' Though that wasn't the entire story. Kaitland had wanted to do something new and different. Jake had known that, too.

"Your pastor thinks you need rest?'' Robert asked, a conniving look on his face.

Instantly wary, for Robert rarely showed such interest in her, she said, "Yes, why?''

Robert reached out and took her hand. "I have a function to attend next week. You know my girlfriend deserted me a year and a half ago and I haven't found anyone to replace her at these social occasions.''

"Is this one of those dinner parties?'' she asked suspiciously.

"Please, Kaitland. Senator Bradley will be there. It's very important I talk to him. He's one of the men against the gambling issue and I need a chance to sway his decision.''

Of course. She should have guessed that Robert's desperate need of her company had to do with his work as a lobbyist.

Kaitland removed her hand from her brother's grip. ''You know I told you after what happened with Senator Richardson that I'd not go to those parties. I hate them.''

''That was an accident. Richardson was drunk. Things like that don't normally happen.''

''So you say. I don't like the way everyone judges me by what I wear, eyeing me, attaching a price tag to my dress. It's demeaning. Besides, I don't have the money to buy a dress for one of those functions.''

''I'll buy you the dress,'' he said, grabbing her hand again. ''And it's only because you don't know anyone that you're uncomfortable. Max Stevens attends those parties sometimes. I bet if he was there you'd attend.''

''If I went with Max, then I might,'' Kaitland agreed. ''But I'm not going with Max. I'm his employee. Therefore, the point is moot.''

Robert's face turned red. ''You'd go with him, yet you won't go with your brother.'' He shot to his feet, his hands fisted. ''Your grandmother brainwashed you against me. It's always been like that, you know. I've always been the outsider.''

Kaitland shot to her feet, too, dismayed at the turn of the conversation, though not surprised. ''That's not true, Robert. You know Mimi loved you just like she did me.''

''No. She loved you, tolerated me. And you're the same way. I come here begging for one small favor and you turn me away like always did. You'd think you'd care a little more about me than that, you who profess to love thy neighbor. Or is that it? You can love your neighbor—'' he motioned toward the mansion ''—but not your own brother.''

With that, he stormed down the path.

Kaitland collapsed back against the bench. It would do no good to chase Robert right now. He'd only argue more. And she did feel a little guilty about what he'd said. She loved her stepbrother. But her grandmother *had* disinherited Robert, and left everything to Kaitland.

However, she was terrified of those parties. Why couldn't Robert understand the burden she carried inside her after that night? She didn't want any part of what had caused the pain and fear in her life. Not again, not just when Max had come back into her life.

If she went to a party like that now, it would only dredge up more hurt and probably get her fired faster than she could blink.

Wearily, her shoulders drooped. ''Why now, Father? It looks like I might have a chance to clear the air between Max and myself and suddenly all of these old problems are making themselves known again. Why?''

With a sigh, she rose from the bench and went back out the gate and toward where Darlene sat with the children. She wondered how she could have thought it would be so easy coming back here, seeing Max and then going on with her life after this temporary job was over. She was afraid this was just the beginning of more momentous things to come.

Chapter Six

Max was avoiding her and the children.

Kaitland juggled the diaper bag as she arranged Maddie in her arms and urged Bobby onward down the long carpeted hall of the building that housed Stevens Inc.

Oh, it had not been obvious at first as Kaitland had adjusted herself to the children's rigorous schedules. But as Maddie and Bobby had settled into a routine, it had quickly become apparent to Kaitland that Max wasn't just missing supper and spending more time than usual at the office. She had no doubt he was doing his best to detach himself from the situation.

The children didn't notice, as they had not grown used to Max yet. But Kaitland noticed. He'd taken to coming up the balcony stairs to his room in the evenings. And if he did pass through the house when she and the children were still up, and happened to run into them, he made some excuse about being tired, or making it an early night and they'd discuss anything that might need discussing at a more opportune time.

And to think, that first night she'd caught him un-
awares, she had only planned to ask him if she could
take the children to the zoo.

Well, he was done avoiding her. She was about to
put an end to that, she thought again determinedly. After all, Max had made the decision to keep the children
until their mother, whoever that was, could be located.
He should at least spend time with them. The children
had no one else. It was up to her to make Max realize
that, whether he wanted to or not. She assured herself
that was her only motivation and that she wasn't upset
that he'd been treating her as if she had the plague
every moment since that first day.

"Door!"

Kaitland, brought abruptly out of her reverie by the
lunging child as she pointed at the door, glanced at the
squirming Maddie in her arms and noted how intently
she examined each door they passed. "Yes, Maddie.
Door. No, Bobby," she admonished gently as the toddler on her right reached toward the leg of a very delicate table with a very expensive china vase sitting on
top of it. "Come on. Take my hand," she urged him,
grabbing hold of his chubby little hand just in time.

She swerved to avoid the cherry-wood table that sat
just outside the main doors leading to Max's office.

Taking a deep breath, she nodded to the receptionist
who was just coming out of a side room, then barged
into the secretary's office before the receptionist could
stop her.

A young girl, no more than twenty-three years old,
Kaitland guessed, looked up from her computer. "May
I help you?" she asked, her glance taking in one child,
then the other. Surprised, Kaitland watched the woman

smile sweetly at both children with a gaze that was soft and loving. Maddie clapped and squealed.

"Go!" Bobby said, reaching toward the secretary.

The secretary winked before glancing back in query at Kaitland.

"I'm here to see Max...Mr. Stevens." Kaitland suddenly realized she didn't even know if Max was in. In the past, he had rarely done the traveling for the company. He had held simple nine-to-five hours unless problems cropped up. Of course, back then, Rand had been around to take care of most of the problems. Now, Max was doing the bulk of the work. Maybe he wasn't here.

"I'm sorry, Jennifer," the receptionist said, coming into the office almost on Kaitland's heels, but the young blonde interrupted her.

"It's all right, Mary." With a small nod, the younger girl dismissed the older woman. "You must be Ms. Summerville?" she inquired politely if a little coolly.

The children were both squirming and despite her resolve, Kaitland suddenly felt like squirming, too. She knew how much Max demanded of his secretaries. How could a woman so young be in such a position of responsibility? Long blond hair coiled in a French twist at the back of her head gave the woman an air of sophistication. Remarkable blue eyes regarded her with wisdom beyond her years. Her long slender hands were more suited to modeling than typing, Kaitland thought. She in her plain jeans and short-sleeve sweater, suddenly realized how underdressed she must look compared to the woman's tailored suit and silk blouse. "Yes, I'm Kaitland Summerville. I know Max said he had to work today, but I needed to see him..."

The girl frowned over Kaitland's use of Max's first

name, causing Kaitland to wonder if maybe there wasn't more going on between the secretary and Max than she realized. She watched as the woman buzzed the office. "Yes, Jennifer?"

Kaitland watched the way the girl's face softened and grew just the tiniest bit dreamy as she responded to Max's query. "Ms. Summerville is here to see you. Would you like me to schedule an appointment with her? Or maybe have her come back..."

"Katie?" The astonishment was quickly covered. "Go ahead and send her in."

Obviously distressed at the sound of Kaitland's nickname on Max's lips, Jennifer nodded toward the door. Maddie squealed again and clapped her hands. Kaitland immediately released Bobby's hand to steady Maddie.

Faster than any toddler should be able to, Bobby toddled around Jennifer's desk.

Kaitland started to race after Bobby, but watched as Jennifer reached down and lifted the boy into her lap. Any jealousy Kaitland had felt melted away as she watched the genuine warmth spread across Jennifer's face. Maddie immediately wiggled from her grasp and followed her brother.

"You like children?" Kaitland smiled when Jennifer glanced up as if startled to see Kaitland still standing there.

"Yes, I do," Jennifer replied. Staring at Kaitland, sizing her up, clearly deciding if she could trust her or not, she finally confided, "I used to work in a day care, was the administrator until it closed down."

Kaitland's disbelief must have shown because Jennifer smiled. "I'd been working there since I was fifteen. My mother owned it. Unfortunately, when she died two years ago, most of the parents and even the staff thought I was too young to run it. We lost too much business and I had to shut the place down.''

''You owned it?'' Kaitland was amazed.

She shrugged. ''My mother owned it. I practically grew up in it. I only ended up here because a friend of mine knew that Rand Stevens needed a temporary secretary while his own was on maternity leave. He liked how levelheaded I was so much he kept me on.''

Kaitland flushed. ''I shouldn't have judged you by your age.''

''Everyone does, even Max.'' Jennifer's frown returned. Kaitland suddenly realized the girl, despite how responsible she appeared to be, was still very young otherwise. She evidently had a huge crush on her boss. Kaitland was almost envious of the sweet innocence that glowed briefly in Jennifer's eyes.

''Well,'' she said, uncomfortable with the knowledge that this young girl liked the same man she herself had almost married. ''Come on Maddie, Bobby. Come with me,'' she coaxed, holding out her hands. She wasn't surprised when the children ignored her.

''Oh, please,'' the secretary said. ''They're no trouble. If you're only going to be a few minutes, you can leave them with me.''

Kaitland didn't miss the girl's hopeful expression. So, she felt threatened by Kaitland, did she? She would have liked to reassure her there was no reason to worry. Max didn't trust her anymore. And there was no chance of that happening in the near future, either. Instead, she nodded. ''Five minutes at the most. But be careful, they're very active.''

Kaitland dropped the diaper bag by the desk and strode in the door. Max was sitting behind his desk, papers spread out everywhere. She was certain they had been placed there in the last few seconds to make him look busy, for she remembered Max *never* let his desk become the least bit unorganized.

The desk was centered in a large, airy room, decorated with green plants everywhere. She'd always liked that about Max's office. Expensive mahogany bookcases lined one wall and on the other end of the office was what he liked to call his negotiating corner. A large fireplace—that was totally electric—was surrounded by soft leather chairs and a tan sofa. It was a place to put someone at ease. Max used to spend a lot of time in that corner when she'd come to visit him. He'd jokingly say they were going to have to find somewhere else to sit and talk, because remembering her sitting there caused no end of distraction when he was trying to make a case for something with one of his business associates.

Reluctantly, she drew her mind away from the fond memories and braced herself for the confrontation ahead. Turning back to Max, she saw he, too, had been staring at the sofa. Did it hold the same memories for him? He focused on her, quickly shuffling his papers to one side of the desk. "What can I do for you, Katie? Is something the matter with the kids? By the way, where are they?"

She smiled. "They're with Jennifer."

"What?" He frowned and stood. "You know I'm trying to keep this quiet. Jennifer won't talk, but running through the offices...and besides, can she even handle those two?"

Kaitland laughed. "She's not a kid," she replied, belying her own thoughts of a minute ago. "Besides, don't you know *anything* about your secretary?"

"What do you mean?" Max had come around the

desk and headed toward the door. At her words, he turned back to her.

"She used to own a day care, or at least, her mother did. She misses it terribly. It was obvious in the way she took to Maddie and Bobby."

"I didn't know," he murmured, slowly strolling over to his desk. Turning, he leaned against it. "So, what are you doing here?"

"I came to invite you to the zoo."

Handing him a spitting cobra would have surprised him less. His mouth fell open. "You *are* kidding, right?"

Kaitland's smile left. "No, I'm *not* kidding. Max, I don't think you've thought out this idea."

"I certainly have," he said. "Kaitland, I appreciate that you think I need a break, but I'm very behind because of Rand's honeymoon. He'll be back in a couple of days or so and I've got to get all of this work caught up."

She realized the work on his desk must be real. Biting her lip in indecision, she glanced at his desk, but then firmed her resolve. The kids needed him, whether he realized it or not, and she was done with him hiding out. "Your needing a break is not what I'm worried about. Actually, it's the kids."

"Are they sick? What is it? You're not making any sense."

"Max!" His eyes widened at her sharp tone. She sighed. "Let me finish."

He nodded.

"You hired me to take care of the kids. I understand that. I love taking care of Maddie and Bobby. However, there is something I think you've neglected in their care."

He frowned and when she didn't say anything more, he finally asked, "What have I neglected?"

"Your presence."

She had definitely caught him by surprise. The hand that was rubbing his chin paused. He stared at her intently, then said, "That's preposterous. They don't even know me."

"Exactly," Kaitland responded. "I'm a nanny, not their mother."

"We're not going through this again, are we, Katie? I told you, I'm not their father."

"But you're the closest thing to a relative they have right now. Don't you see that?" she pleaded, her hands going out in supplication. "I'm temporary. I'll leave soon. But you'll be left behind. Think how hard that will be on the children. They need to bond with you, have someone to hold on to until their mother can be located. And that someone should be you, not me. You do remember I have a job to go back to in a few weeks, don't you?"

"But what do I know about kids? I'm a bachelor," Max complained helplessly. "That's why I hired you."

"I know that, Max. But what would you have done when we had children?" she asked softly, trying to make a point.

His eyes darkened. "That would've been different. I could have learned day by day."

She smiled. "Tell me why you refused to let them be turned over to Child Services?"

Max pushed away from his desk and paced toward the fireplace. "I didn't want them separated."

"But why?"

Casting her a harassed look, he replied, "They need each other... I don't know. You had to see them that morning when I found them. They are part of each other, depending on each other. I can't explain how it is to be a twin. I just *know* how it is and it would've been cruel to separate them.''

"I agree."

"Then why did you ask me?" he replied.

"To remind you it was you who wanted them living at your house, you who went out of your way to make sure you could keep them."

Max sighed, but Kaitland wasn't done. "And to remind you that whether you want to admit it or not, you feel something for them."

"I'm not afraid to admit that," he grumbled.

Kaitland thought that was at the heart of his problem. He didn't want to care. He wanted to hide in his own world where he could be nice, have fun, but have no close attachments.

Why, she'd never understood, but later, after their breakup, she'd wondered if there wasn't more driving Max than just the thought of those pictures. He'd never tried to work it out, never tried to find out why.

She didn't say anything about his reasons for avoiding the children. Instead, she said, "I didn't think you were. But just imagine how much easier it'll be for the children if you're there when I leave. They need someone steady so they won't be hurt."

Walking over to where he was standing, she looked up into his dark brown eyes and said, "I'm not asking much, Max. I know you're a very busy person. But if Rand is going to be gone a couple more days, what will it hurt to play hooky? He won't know. And I doubt he'd care if you did. You've held up the business admirably the past couple of years. You've taken on many responsibilities, just like you have with those kids out in the reception area. What will it hurt to cut loose for a few hours, escort us to the zoo and have some fun?''

She smiled when his lips twitched. That was a sign he was weakening. She knew him too well. "It's not like I'm asking you to adopt them," she drawled. "Just get to know them, spend a couple of hours a day with them.''

"If I agree, will it keep you out of the office and away from the possible exposure to the media that's always lurking here?" he asked seriously.

A slow smile spread across her face and Max looked just a little stunned. Had it been that long since he'd seen her smile? she wondered. "I can guarantee it, Maxwell Edward Stevens," she replied. "And you've just given me a weapon. If you start neglecting us, I promise to come down here and bug you until our pictures are plastered in every magazine west of the Mississippi!''

His lips curved into a reluctant smile. "And you would, too, wouldn't you, Kaitland Amanda Summerville.''

Grinning sweetly, she didn't answer. He knew she'd never go to the press, with his hating them as much as he did.

"Okay, che'rie, you win, despite your obvious lies. Let me straighten that up—" he motioned toward the desk "—and we'll go. Luckily, today was a light load. No appointments, just paperwork that needed catching up on and I decided to do it here..." He winced as if suddenly realizing what he was revealing.

"To avoid me," she supplied, refusing to let him see how much his reasons for frequenting the office hurt. "But we've put an end to that," she said lightly, letting him read into her words that she thought it was only the kids he was avoiding and not her. "So, I'll expect to see you at home around the children more often."

She turned toward the door. "Well, I'd better go check on the demolition team—"

"Katie." His hand on her arm stopped her. Biting her lip to hold in the hurt, she did her best to put on a smile.

"It's okay, really, Max."

"Look, I'm sorry. I know this is difficult."

Letting go of her arm, he ran a hand wearily through his hair. "This was one reason why I wanted someone else. It would have been easier—"

"Not to see each other again?" she asked, the smile still intact though her face felt as set as concrete.

"Yes. We had broken it off, gotten on with our lives. It would have been a lot easier not to be thrown together again."

"If we really had gotten on with our lives, Max, if we had actually gotten over the past and were living again, would our being together really hurt this much?"

Max opened his mouth to reply but he never got the chance. A loud crash on the other side of the door held his words within.

Both Max and Kaitland stared at each other in shock then in unison groaned.

"The kids!" Max said.

"The kids," Kaitland confirmed.

Chapter Seven

Max jerked open the door to his office. "What's going on out here?" he said, then stopped, his stunned shock turning to dismay.

"Oh dear," Kaitland said, scooting past Max and going toward the children.

Max wasn't surprised at the state of the office. Not really. Hadn't he learned since the children's arrival in his life what to expect?

"I should have warned you, Jennifer, that Maddie likes plants," Kaitland said. "That's not poisonous, is it?"

Maddie, sitting near the far end of the office, was covered in dirt and stuffing a leaf in her mouth as Jennifer tried to clean up the mess.

Seeing Max, Bobby squealed and made a beeline for him. Absently, Max lifted Bobby into his arms. The little boy promptly dropped his head to Max's shoulder.

The feeling Max had been running from all week was immediately present again. These kids had the power no one else had, to slip past his guard and wind their way around his heart.

Something soft and squishy, grainy, touched his chest. "Well, I guess I'll be leaving work now instead of later," Max said resignedly.

"What... Oh, no, Max!" Kaitland sighed.

Max looked down at the handful of dirt Bobby had been holding in his hand. Half was down the child's trousers, the rest smeared on Max's jacket and shirt.

Cutting his eyes toward the toddler he held, he was met by an impish grin. Then the wetness came. "He's leaking—again."

Kaitland rushed over. "I'm so sorry. I don't know why he keeps leaking out of his diapers every time you hold him..."

"Not to worry," Max said. "I have some casual clothes in the office. I wear them sometimes when I have somewhere to go after work and don't want to run home and change. So, while I clean up, how about cleaning these two up?"

Without waiting for a reply, he went back into his office and headed for the private bathroom. He hoped this was not a sign of what was to come. He'd never met two little kids who could get into more trouble than those two. With a small smile, he remembered some of his and Rand's antics. Well, almost no one, he amended. He and his brother had certainly turned his parents' hair gray.

But these were only babies. And he was beginning to think Bobby had some delicate condition. Every time he picked that child up, Bobby spit up or had an accident on him. Kaitland didn't seem to think there was anything wrong with Bobby. Maybe if Max spent more time around the children, he would find out that

Bobby didn't get sick every time he picked up the boy. Maybe it was just coincidence since he'd held him so little.

He pulled his dark slacks and green pullover off the hanger and slipped into them. Then he washed off all traces of dirt and grime. It wasn't often he wore casual clothes anymore. He had started keeping an outfit at work when Kaitland and he had been dating. She would often show up just as he was getting off and suggest some outrageous place to go where a suit would definitely be out of place. After their breakup, he had continued to keep clothes here out of habit.

Kaitland.

Even now his heart ached for her. She was so beautiful, so sweet, so generous. He wanted to take her in his arms and kiss her and tell her the past could be forgotten.

But it couldn't.

Kaitland was right. The past was like some big silent monster than hung between them.

Arranging his suit on a hanger, he gave himself one last check. He reminded himself that no matter what, the past was not going away. There was no way to heal the hurt, was there? Too much pain and damage had passed between them for him to reach out and pull her into his arms and offer comfort. *Father, what am I going to do? Why this temptation now?*

Max didn't wait for an answer. Instead, he took out his soiled suit and laid it over the couch.

He buzzed Phil, his driver, on the phone. "Meet me downstairs in five minutes."

Going out to his secretary's office, he was glad to see both children being held by Jennifer and Kaitland. "Jennifer, have my suit cleaned, please, and have housekeeping come clean up this mess. If anyone has any questions, direct them to my vice president, Hunter. You'll be able to reach me later at home. If it's an emergency, page me.'' He indicated the small pager on his belt.

Holding out his hands, he watched as Maddie lunged at him, just as he knew she would. Contrary to what Kaitland thought, Max spent a lot of time watching her and the children as they played. He knew Maddie loved to lunge, liked plants and was the leader in mischief. Bobby liked to stick things in his mouth, but was not as likely to dance as Maddie. He loved to be held, whereas Maddie liked to be free and wild. So, he expected the lunge and caught Maddie up in his arms. ''Ready to go, Katie?''

She picked up the diaper bag. ''Ready.''

They left the office and started down the hall. She nodded to three people they passed and was confused by how cautious they were to respond, hurrying off to another office or disappearing behind doors.

It was unusually quiet, only Maddie babbling and Bobby noisily sucking his thumb. ''So much for prudence,'' Max finally murmured dryly.

''I didn't remember you having this large a staff,'' Kaitland agreed, nodding again to a woman they passed.

''That all of them had so many errands to run at least,'' Max added as they reached the elevators. ''I imagine I'm going to add greatly to the rumor mill.''

''They won't take it to the papers, will they?'' Kaitland glanced warily around at the secretaries as they went to the copier or peeked out of offices. She could hear the low hum of conversation as a possible explanation came to her. "There weren't this many people around when I came up," she added.

"The people that work on this floor are picked for discretion as well as skills. No, they won't go to the paper," he added darkly. "If they value their jobs."

The private elevator opened. Max stepped back to let Kaitland pass him. He stepped in behind her. "As for the number of people on the floor...I imagine every person on this end of the building was on the phone right after you passed, calling everyone on Rand's end of the building to inform them that an unknown woman—for those who don't remember you—was seen entering my office with twins."

Kaitland blushed when he confirmed her suspicions. "I'm sorry, Max. I guess I forgot how much attention you attract."

Max chuckled and finally met Kaitland's gaze. "Che'rie, it's not me. Anyone that's single who has a beautiful woman show up at his door toting twins who resemble him in coloring would be speculated about. Just relax. It's none of their business. I don't have to explain myself."

Kaitland shook her head.

"What?" Max asked, bouncing Maddie when she squirmed in his arms.

"You. I wish I could be as easygoing about what people thought about me. How do you do it?"

"I've had practice. There's an article at least once a month in the papers about me, wondering about my job, my life, my brother, or my private life. You learn to ignore it."

"It never bothered you?"

Max shrugged, chucking Maddie under the chin when she hit him on the face and burbled something excitedly. "That's right, che'rie," he murmured, then said to Kaitland. "Occasionally. But not enough that I'm going to make myself sick over it. The only time it really matters is if it hurts my family. And then, I can be very unforgiving if it is done by someone I know."

"I remember Rand telling me once about an old friend selling articles about your childhood..."

"Old friend is right. I let him know how displeased I was. He got angry. It ruined our friendship, even though later I did apologize for my temper. It was still wrong of him, though."

"He shouldn't have betrayed your trust. But you need to forget it, Max. Forgetting is part of forgiving," she murmured.

"Private information that hits the papers is hard to forget." Max was thinking of the last time he'd been ill over any upsetting news. That had been with Kaitland five years ago. Katie's pictures had been the last time he'd been ill over what people thought. And that had been personal, it didn't deal with papers at all, though some photographer had been responsible for destroying his future.

The elevator opened in the private parking lot where the company's executives parked. Max stepped out and started toward his car.

"We need to take my car," Katie said.

Max glanced to his limo, which was just pulling up.

"You don't have car seats," she explained.

"Car seats? I hadn't thought."

"Well, I keep them in my car since I'm the one who usually does any running with the children. I suppose we could put the seats in your car. But let's face it, the press know that car. They don't know mine."

"A good idea," he replied.

Kaitland watched as he walked over to the limo. Relieved, she let out a sigh. Max had been withdrawn even though he'd agreed to go with her to the zoo. She wasn't sure what he was thinking, or what he had wanted to ask, but she did know she was afraid of that faraway look he had in his eyes. It meant he was thinking about things she didn't want to confront right now.

The limo pulled off and Max returned. She gratefully led the way to her car, a white compact. She noticed how old it looked compared to Max's sleek Mercedes that was parked in the garage back at the house. She was a little embarrassed to have him see this vehicle.

"What happened to your other car?" he asked.

"It proved to be too expensive," she replied lightly.

Max looked at her, his eyes narrowing. "Too expensive?"

She shrugged. Taking Bobby, she easily slipped him into his car seat and buckled him in. Max had a more difficult time with Maddie. She was glad it distracted him from her answer, though, or she thought it did, until he closed the door and looked over the hood at her.

"I don't like asking this, Katie, but just how tight did your grandmother's illness leave you?"

Kaitland smiled grimly. "Since you don't like asking it, you'll be relieved to know I have no intention of answering. Shall we go?" She held up the keys, grinning. She knew he didn't like her driving. He'd always complained she went too fast.

He slid into the passenger's seat while she got behind the wheel. "You sure you don't want me to drive?" he asked.

"Absolutely," she replied. "I thought you liked being chauffeured," she added.

"By a chauffeur," he muttered.

Her laughter tinkled out in the small car. Maddie immediately echoed the sound. Bobby just grunted, which caused Max to smile.

"It's not far to the zoo so I don't see why you're worried," Kaitland said.

"I'm not," he said, and she knew he was lying.

"So," Kaitland said once they were on the interstate, "have you heard anything from the private investigator you hired?"

"Nothing good." Max adjusted in his seat, turning a little so he could see her. Kaitland unconsciously tensed. Having Max so close was not something she'd bargained on when they'd entered the car. She could smell his spicy aftershave, almost feel the breaths he was taking as he faced her. Memories swamped her but she forced them to the recesses of her mind.

"As far as Dugan can tell, there were several births in the area that might just be our person. He's narrowed it down to eighteen—assuming the woman who had the children wasn't married. We're guessing that's the case since she left the kids with me instead of the father. There were thirty-one people he was checking out. We'll have to get lucky soon."

"Why would it take so long?" she questioned, easily flowing in and out of traffic as she traversed the busy road.

"Some had moved from the area, a few were given up for adoption. It's hard to track down that type of information and confirm it by talking with these people. Plus, he had a few favors to call in to get some of this information in the first place."

Kaitland glanced in her rearview mirror at the two children playing contentedly in their seats. "Why would someone run like that, giving up her children?"

Max was quiet a long time. "Maybe she thought they'd have a better life with someone who had money."

"But that's awful," Kaitland replied.

"Not if she believes that person would provide for her children when she couldn't."

Kaitland shook her head. "I can't imagine having to give my children away."

"If the mother was sick, or dying, maybe that was the most generous thing she could have done."

Kaitland sighed. "They miss her, you know."

Max didn't comment. He was looking out the window, gazing off in the distance.

She continued, "Some nights they wake up fussy and just don't want anything to do with me. I notice it more in Bobby. I've found putting the two of them in the same crib helps. They're pretty stable otherwise, but it's those little things. The second day on the job, Maddie just kept crying for her mother, right in the middle of eating a plant or playing patty-cake. She'd sniffle and call out, 'Mama'. It's so sad."

"We'll find her," Max said in a low tone. "We'll find out why she had to leave, help her if we can. I won't let her desert these children if we can help her."

Kaitland took the exit to Baker, a small suburb between Baton Rouge and Zachary, and in minutes was at the zoo.

"You know, they've been rather good," Max commented as they climbed out of the car.

"Very good," Kaitland agreed.

They carried the children to the gate, where they

bought tickets. Inside, Max surprised Kaitland by taking the stroller and strapping Bobby in. When he reached for Maddie, their hands touched. Kaitland couldn't help sucking in a sharp breath. His skin was so warm, his hands so masculine against her own feminine size.

Their eyes met. His eyes warmed until they were suddenly banked by the memories of their past. "Let me just strap this little girl in," Max said.

Kaitland walked on ahead looking at the peacocks. Max was right behind her.

"You know, it's been years since I've been to the zoo."

He paused near the Louisiana State University mascot's cage and allowed the children to look at the tiger. "I'd forgotten they kept Mike the Tiger here," he said.

"If it's been very long since you've been here, you're in for a surprise. They have elephant rides, and a hands-on room. It's really fun. I love to come here myself."

Max sighed. "It's always going to be there, isn't it?"

Kaitland knew he was referring to their past. "I don't want it to be, Max. But I don't know what to do to help you get over your hurt."

"I don't know what to do, either," Max said. "You're a great woman, Kaitland. But what you did…"

She waited to see what he said. It hurt her that he still didn't believe her.

"Why, Katie? Why?" he asked, the words torn from him.

Kaitland ached with remorse. "Would you believe

me if I said it was an accident? I went upstairs looking for my brother and the senator was there.''

"I can maybe believe that, but why did you let him kiss you. I *saw* the pictures. You and he were kissing. He had you on the bed. Katie, I'm not blind.''

"No, you're not, are you?" she said sadly. It did no good to try to explain. He didn't believe her. And besides, she was ashamed of what had happened and feared the disbelief or coolness that would enter his eyes when she told him everything. Still, in her own hurt, she added, "Maybe you could have trusted me and asked me before dropping the pictures in my lap.''

"And what would you have said? It had been over a month, Katie. Why didn't you come to me immediately? I mean, what was I to think? This happens. A month later I get the pictures and a blackmail note. I confront you and you don't deny the pictures? What was I suppose to believe?" He paused, then, "You know how often weirdos try to blackmail my family. Remember, this has happened before. That's why I now have Jennifer instead of my last secretary. The woman was saying it was my child she carried and was intending to blackmail me. Of course, we found out who had planned the extortion. But can't you see, Katie, how common this kind of thing is in my life?''

"Is it common for the woman you love to try and blackmail you?''

"I don't know. There was only one woman I'd ever loved.''

Loved. Past tense. Her heart constricted with pain. Kaitland pasted a smile on her face. "Well, that's all in the past. I just want us to be friends. Can't we manage that?''

"I don't know.''

Kaitland glanced at him. "Look. It's obvious you no longer have feelings for me. That's fine. But you were always so much fun to be around. Can't we just enjoy that?"

Finally, Max nodded.

Forcing herself to smile brightly, Kaitland said, "So, how about an elephant ride?" She would do her best to be the happy, easygoing woman he remembered. Maybe, in time, he would see she wanted nothing to do with him except to bury the past and be friends again while she was working for him.

A slow smile spread across his face. "Just let me run back to the souvenir shop and buy a camera. I think Maddie and Bobby will need a picture of this for later."

She laughed at the boyish look in his eyes. "You just want a camera in case I fall off."

His grin widened, the past temporarily forgotten as both Kaitland and Max focused on the children and making today a memorable one. "That, too. I know how clumsy you can be." He chuckled. "And I'd love to get it on film. Now stay there. If you're good, I'll bring us all back some cotton candy."

"Oh, Max, I don't think that would be a good idea."

Max paused on the sidewalk, stepping out of the way as a group of schoolkids trudged past with their teachers. When they were gone he stepped back over to Kaitland. "Why not? I know you love cotton candy."

Kaitland smiled, the last of the tension finally leaving her. "Of course I love cotton candy. But remember the kids?"

"I'm sure they'll love it," Max reassured.

"I'm sure they will, too. But they'll make a mess."

Max glanced down at the children, then shrugged.

"They're calm enough now being pushed around out here in the open. I think we can keep the cotton candy off them."

"It wasn't them I was worrying about."

"Come on, Katie. Where's your sporting adventure? You wanted to go to the zoo. No zoo trip is complete without cotton candy. Are you going to let two little kids intimidate you?"

Famous last words, she thought, and smiled wanly.

Chapter Eight

"What happened to you?"

"Rand! Welcome home." Max stuck out his hand and grasped his brother's hand. Rand, who had been eyeing the children, now looked down at his hand in disgust. Holding his hand up, he studied it as if some foreign creature had attached itself to it. "What is so sticky? And why is your hair sticking up in tufts? And, if I may be so bold, who is the child... Kaitland..."

Rand's voice fell away as Kaitland entered behind Max. Max watched Rand's eyes go to the twins, then back to Kaitland as if speculating, then negating what his mind was conjuring up.

"Hello, Rand," Kaitland said softly, shifting Maddie from one hip to the other. She reached out with her other arm and took the sleeping child from Max. "I'll just go put them down for a nap, Max," she said and turned toward the stairs.

Max didn't like the incredulous look on Rand's face. "Let me explain," he said. "It's a long story."

A curious smile crossed Rand's face. "I'd like to

hear you try." Going toward the den, Max studied his brother as they walked.

"You look tanned and fit," he said. Rand did indeed look good again. Beige pants and a green shirt, more casual than what Max was wearing, showed his body had filled out again and his clothes no longer hung on a gaunt frame. They looked more like identical twins once more.

"I had a wonderful time," Rand told him. "But that's not what we're talking about so don't try to change the subject."

Max rolled his eyes. Rand was only minutes older but could really act superior sometimes. "You were wondering about Kaitland," Max said, going into the den.

"Actually, I was wondering about those children *and* Kaitland."

"Like I said, it's a long story." Max seated himself on the leather sofa, stretching out his feet in front of him. He was hot, tired and covered in cotton candy. All he wanted to do was bathe. Kaitland had been right. Only someone eligible for psychiatric care would attempt to feed sticky cotton candy to toddlers.

But instead of a bath, he now had to explain to his brother who had arrived back two days early, not that he'd taken off work, but that he'd taken off work to bond with two kids who weren't even his. This was going to be just great.

"The babies were left on my doorstep, so to speak."

"On the doorstep?" Rand asked, shock evident in his voice.

"Well, actually, they were left at the bottom of the stairs on the patio."

"How did someone get in?"

Max shrugged. "The security was off that night. It was Sarah's night out and she remembers leaving it off."

"Do you have any idea who…"

Again Max shrugged, easily accepting how flabbergasted Rand was at the explanation. "You know I'm not promiscuous. I sent for a nanny, deciding to do nothing drastic until I figured out what was going on."

"There wasn't a note or anything?"

"Oh, yeah, brother," he said, his accent thickening. "There was a note. *Mais oui,*" he said, nodding again for emphasis. "It was an introduction to Madeline Renée and Maxwell Robert."

"One of them is actually named Max?" Rand sounded as if he was strangling on his own voice.

"We call him by his middle name—Bobby."

"There's no chance they can be yours?" Rand asked, though earlier Max was certain Rand had discounted that notion.

"No chance at all."

"And they're not, um…" He looked uncomfortable as his voice trailed off.

Max's face hardened. "They're not Katie's, either."

"I wondered. They do have a look about them that reminds me of the old Katie, that look of mischief she used to wear."

Max stiffened, the old pain rearing its head. "No. They're no relation to either one of us."

"So, why haven't you sent them to a social worker by now if that's the case?" Rand asked when Max added nothing else to their identity.

"I couldn't do that, Rand," Max said. "The mother left them with me for some reason. I have Dugan Lawrence out looking for her. I need to care for them, at least until we have an explanation. Besides, if I sent the children to the state system, chances are they'd be broken up and sent to different foster parents. The kids can't handle that. They shouldn't have to handle that," he amended. "Just think what it was like for us as kids when Mom or Dad put us in separate rooms to punish us. I can't imagine any kids going through that kind of separation right after losing their mom."

"Since when have you become so paternal?" Rand asked wryly.

"I'm not," Max argued. "Just concerned for those kids." Though he did remember how awful it had been that last year his mom and dad had been alive, and how Sarah had done her best to give Max and Rand the stability they had needed. Maybe, Max silently admitted, that was behind some of his reasoning to help these kids. He didn't want them going through the insecurity of being tossed about. True, the children's parents were gone, not going through problems the way his had been.

But still, the memories, the one thing he hadn't shared with Rand, of how frustrated and angry—and scared—he'd felt when his mom had gotten tired of the newspaper articles and decided she needed to get away from everyone—including him and Rand. And his father, worried about failing her, insisting it was all his fault, convincing her to go on one last vacation to try to work it all out. Then their deaths and feeling bereft, alone in the world...

"So, you weren't carrying a little boy in your arms when you walked in."

Max shrugged.

"What's in your hair?" Rand asked.

"Cotton candy."

Rand smiled. "Let me get this straight. You just had to help carry the children earlier, too, when you were at...?"

"The zoo," Max confessed defensively.

"Ah, the zoo." Rand nodded gravely as if Max's explanation didn't border on the bizarre. "*With* two children and Kaitland," he added, nodding again.

"Kaitland is their nanny." Rand was enjoying every minute of this, Max thought, disgusted.

Rand lowered his head, rubbing his chin in amusement.

"Don't say anything," Max warned.

Rand only shook his head, then ignored his brother's warning and went on. "This is the same sweet, beautiful Kaitland who was caught in a compromising position with a senator, isn't it, Max?"

"You know it is. And I know you had trouble believing it when it happened. So, don't goad me. I don't want to discuss that, by the way." he added.

Rand, as usual, ignored him and continued. "But you're letting Kaitland work here, with these children you're worried about. Don't you think she wants to discuss the past?"

Max frowned. "We've come to an understanding. There will be nothing from the past brought up. We're just going to try to be friends. As a matter of fact, Katie is only temporarily a nanny. I told her as soon as Elizabeth got back, she'd be able to help me out until I can find someone regular. It would only be a few days at most. I'm sure by then we will have found the mother."

Rand was already shaking his head. "I'm afraid that's not possible, Max. Elizabeth's pregnant."

Max stared, stunned. "But she can't have babies.

You told me the doctor said the damage caused by her ex-fiancé when he pushed her down the stairs had scarred her permanently."

"The doctor was wrong."

Max's shock turned to joy and a huge smile spread across his face. "Congratulations." He jumped up to shake Rand's hand. Rand stared at it distastefully. "We'll forgo another handshake until you can wash up. But thank you for the well-wishes. As for Elizabeth's barrenness... It's true there was a lot of damage when her ex-fiancé shoved her down the stairs. But evidently not as much as the doctor thought. She's definitely pregnant, morning sickness and all. But I'm not allowing her to work until she's further along. I'm afraid for both her and the baby."

"I understand completely," Max said.

"What I would suggest is to keep Kaitland on."

Max stared in disbelief. "But I can't do that."

Rand raised an eyebrow and Max almost groaned. Rand was always getting Max in trouble with that look. "Don't even say it. I'm not keeping Katie here. I have things that need doing. I don't want the distractions."

"So, she's still a distraction?" Rand asked, looking amused.

"I didn't mean distraction," Max amended, though thinking about her soft hand and gentle smile, he realized she was indeed a distraction—and more. *Obsession* was the word that came to mind.

"It would be easier on the kids if you kept her," Rand said. "And don't forget, she's an emergency foster parent—or used to be."

Max scowled.

Rand chuckled. "Face it, brother. You're gonna

have to put your feelings aside—good or bad—and let Kaitland stay. You need her.''

Rand stood. ''I'm going to go wash my hands. I suggest you shower and then I'd like a report on who's running the business while you've been running your life.''

He left.

Max walked over to a mirror and stared at his reflection. Rand was right. He looked as though he'd been mowed over by a crazy Weed Eater. His hair was sticking up every which way. His shirt had stains on it. And his face. His eyes had a haunted look that he didn't like one bit.

Going to the door, he headed up the stairs toward his room. He would not allow himself to care for Katie again.

No way. No how. Out of the question.

Trust must be part of the relationship. And he didn't trust her. Well, maybe he did, with the kids, *temporarily*. But not with his heart.

''May I come in?''

Kaitland glanced over to where a short perky redhead stood at the door. A soft tentative smile creased the woman's face and her eyes glowed with kindness.

''I'm just changing diapers,'' Kaitland said. ''When Bobby and Maddie go down, it's for the count.''

Elizabeth laughed, the soft, sweet sound quiet in the large room. ''I didn't think kids this age ever took a nap. I'm Elizabeth.''

''Rand's wife,'' she acknowledged. At Elizabeth's surprised look, she added, ''I read the paper. And even if I didn't, Max has told me all about what a miracle worker you are.''

"Max doesn't have much faith in his brother."

"Oh, no," Kaitland corrected. "He does. He thinks Rand is very intelligent, and when Max met you, he knew Rand couldn't let you get away."

Elizabeth chuckled again. Kaitland placed a blanket over the kids, took the diapers to the pail then went to the rest room to wash her hands. When she was done, she motioned to the sitting room off the main nursery room. "How can I help you?"

Elizabeth shrugged and seated herself next to Kaitland. "I saw the children when you passed earlier and was just curious."

"They're not Max's," Kaitland said, not wanting Elizabeth to think ill of her brother-in-law.

Elizabeth smiled. "I know that. Max isn't the type to hide kids in the wings."

"Someone left them on his doorstep. He hired me to be their nanny until he can locate the mother."

Elizabeth made a shocked sound in her throat.

"I think he's planning on asking you to watch the kids now that you're back," Kaitland said.

"I'm afraid he'll have to find someone else," Elizabeth told her. "I'll be glad to help, but I can tell you right now, Rand will say no. You see, I'm pregnant. We never thought I could conceive after some other problems." A dark cloud crossed her features momentarily then they brightened again. "Now Rand won't let me do anything. He wanted to extend our honeymoon two more months so I would take it easy. I promised if we returned home, I wouldn't lift a finger until we were certain I wasn't going to miscarry."

"I can tell you're very happy about the child."

"I am. Now, correct me if I'm wrong, but don't you usually run the day care at my church?"

Kaitland smiled. "I do. I didn't think you remembered me."

Elizabeth rolled her eyes. "I once tried to find you to introduce Rand to you. I was desperate to help Rand, and thought if he met a nice woman it would bring him out of his depression."

"I think he met the only one he wanted to," Kaitland replied, staring at Elizabeth's glow. "And vice versa."

Elizabeth nodded. "True. But at the time I didn't want to be involved with a patient. You see, I was his occupational therapist."

"I see," Kaitland said.

"And you," Elizabeth asked, grinning. "How do you feel about being involved with your boss?"

Kaitland paled. "It's not what you think."

Elizabeth's smile collapsed as she obviously realized she'd said something a bit too outrageous and had struck some unseen nerve. "I'm sorry. I shouldn't have said that. To me, it's just so obvious in your eyes when you say Max's name..."

Kaitland smoothed the creases in her cotton pants, refusing to meet Elizabeth's eyes. "Max and I were once engaged. It didn't work out."

There was a pause. "But you're working for him now."

"I took the job hoping God could heal the breach between us. I've been in limbo for years over things that happened between us five years ago. I had hoped to see Max, heal the breach and part as friends."

"But that hasn't happened."

Kaitland shook her head, unable to believe she was telling Elizabeth this. They'd spoken in church before, but had never been involved socially. "Please don't repeat this to Max."

Elizabeth reached out and took her hand. "Of course not. It's painful to still love someone who doesn't realize it."

"Oh, I don't love him," Kaitland protested.

"Don't you?" Elizabeth asked. "Well, it doesn't matter. These Stevens men can be real thickheaded. But I'd say if you're still here, that must be a good sign that you can handle them."

"But I was only supposed to be here until you showed up. I imagine when Rand shoots down Max's idea, he'll find someone else. So, either way, I'm sure to be gone."

"Ahem." Both women turned to see Max strolling through the door. "I hope I'm not barging in on a tête-à-tête, but I need to talk to Kaitland."

Elizabeth stood. "No welcome for me?"

Max smiled, momentarily distracted. Opening his arms, he allowed Elizabeth to step into them. She squealed when he hefted her up and spun her around.

Kaitland's heart squeezed painfully as she watched the interaction.

Planting a big smack on Elizabeth's cheek, Max said, "Welcome home, sis. If Rand gets too cautious with you over your delicate condition, you just let me know."

"I just might take you up on that," Elizabeth whispered, then hugged him back.

"Don't be swinging my wife around like that," Rand drawled, leaning against the doorjamb with a smile that said he wasn't totally serious.

Both Elizabeth and Max groaned.

Rand ignored them. "Come along, Elizabeth. The plane ride was long. You need a nap."

"Tyrant," she muttered, bringing a smile to Max's face.

"You're just learning that?" he asked innocently.

Elizabeth smiled and stepped over to Rand.

Rand nodded to Kaitland, slipped his arm around Elizabeth's waist and started out the door. Kaitland could tell by the way Rand's features softened that everyone else in the room was forgotten as he fussed over his wife.

When it was quiet again, Max turned back to Kaitland. Her stomach knotted painfully. She was about to be offered her last check and shown the door.

It was time to go and nothing really had been solved. Max had agreed to try to be friends and they'd spent time together, but she still had all of these feelings, feelings she hadn't recognized until they'd been riding the elephant together at the zoo, holding the children in their laps. She wanted more, wanted something special with Max.

But that was impossible, she admonished.

Still, it was there, the wanting, needing, yearning. Oh, why did that senator have to attack her? And who had taken those photos? Why hadn't she come to Max to tell him about the incident? If she had, she'd likely have her own children by now. Little ones just like the two in the other room, probably twins, since twins ran in her family, just as in Max's.

"So, what did you need to talk to me about?" she asked him.

Max paced to the balcony doors and stared out. "Elizabeth is pregnant."

Just as she'd feared. "She told me. We'd met once

or twice before, though I wasn't sure she would remember me. I do go to a fairly large church.''

Max laughed. "A hundred and fifty isn't large."

"For Zachary it is."

"Granted. At any rate, Elizabeth is pregnant and Rand has promised to have my hide if I dare propose to Elizabeth the idea of working with the children."

Kaitland smiled, though it was tinged with sadness. Rand just might say something like that. But she had a feeling Max was exaggerating. "I understand. Have you contacted the employment agency yet?"

Max turned around in surprise. "Are you that eager to leave? I thought since the kids knew you, it might be best if you stayed until we locate the mother."

Kaitland's heart soared, but she did her best to keep her facial expression neutral. "I'd like that very much. Maddie and Bobby are a wonder. I've enjoyed being with them."

"And you need the money," Max stated.

Kaitland nodded stiffly. "Yes, Max. I need the money."

Concern etched his forehead. "Why won't you tell me how much you owe? I'd be glad to help you out."

"Don't do it, Max."

"Do what?"

"Don't go snooping. We're no longer involved. This is strictly business. You have no right to ask questions about my life now."

"Who said I would do that?" he asked innocently.

"I know you. Once you get on the trail of something that interests you, you don't let up."

She saw something like a flash of pain in his eyes, then a melancholy look that lingered. "I don't, do I?"

She shrugged, uncomfortable, looking away.

"I thought we'd agreed to be friends," he said.

"Friends don't confide everything," she replied.

Max sighed. Finally, he crossed the room. The sofa gave as he seated himself by her. Kaitland felt his near-ness, wanted to turn into his arms where she had once found comfort, but knew she'd run into a brick wall if she did. So, she sat, waiting to hear what Max said.

"With Elizabeth pregnant, it's doubly important we get along. Rand is afraid she'll lose the baby, and any undue tension might affect her adversely."

Kaitland smiled. "You're as bad as Rand. Elizabeth is stronger than she looks."

"She was almost killed a few months ago."

It was Kaitland's turn to stare, shocked. "What?"

"We kept it out of the newspapers. But an ex-fiancé caught up with her and attacked her. She was shot. She lived, but barely."

"I had no idea."

"We want it that way. You know how people pursue anything to do with our name. I'm only taking you into my confidence because you won't spread the information to the news."

"Thank you."

"I still trust you, Katie."

"A little."

"As much as I can," he replied, and there was gen-uine pain in his voice. "But this isn't about us. This is about Elizabeth."

"I understand. I won't do anything to worry Eliza-beth," Kaitland agreed.

"Thank you," Max said, standing. "I'll have your paycheck on the desk this evening."

"And I still get Sunday off?"

"No problem. Sarah has agreed to help in your absence.'' He walked to the door. ''With Rand back, things should settle down some and one free day is only reasonable.''

''Thank you.''

With sadness, Kaitland watched him leave. She knew he still didn't trust her. He was back to treating her coolly, as if she was an employee again, too. *Why, God? What must I do to make him trust me?* Even as she asked, Kaitland realized there was nothing she could *do* to make Max trust her. She'd just have to hope the longer she was around Max the more he would come to see she wasn't what he thought.

And then what?

Could there ever be more?

Kaitland wondered about that a long time. With a slow smile, she decided Max's keeping her on as nanny was a good beginning.

Chapter Nine

"Marjorie! Come on in." Kaitland wiped her hands on her shorts, and opened the door wider. "I was just finishing some scrubbing in the kitchen, then I have to work on my car. Unfortunately, it gave out just as I got back from the store."

She glanced at her watch, then at the pretty redhead in front of her. "So, what's up?"

Marjorie smiled, shook her head ruefully and strolled into the house. "You should get rid of that piece of junk in the driveway and get you a new car, if you want my opinion. And I just stopped by to visit. Can't I visit an old friend?"

Kaitland laughed, walked back into the kitchen to finish her work and replied over her shoulder, "There's always more with you, isn't there, though?"

"Shame on you, Kaitland. Not *always*."

Kaitland finished wiping down the stove she had decided to scrub to take out her frustrations on before she went out to try to fix the car. It was better, she had learned, to be relaxed when you tackled something with the car, and she certainly hadn't been relaxed when the radiator had sprung a leak in her driveway just as she'd pulled in from shopping. "So, you want to know what I'm up to?" Kaitland asked. "Just like any good reporter who loves the Stevens, you've come to find out why I'm out there."

Marjorie laughed again. "I'd give anything for the scoop, Kaitland. But I would never come to you." Kaitland turned from the stove in time to see her friend's expression turn serious. "Yes, I'd heard a woman was at the Stevens' house, and people are wondering. I called to ask you to lunch and found out you weren't at the day care for the next three weeks, and put two and two together. You're out at Max's, aren't you?"

Kaitland smiled. Marjorie might be a reporter for a local newspaper, but she'd never before printed anything without Kaitland's permission. And she was sure the woman wouldn't start now. "I'm working for him temporarily, that's all I can say."

Marjorie nodded. "Are you okay with this? I mean, I know bills have been tight, but if they're so tight you have to go back working for him after everything that happened…"

"It's an opportunity to get over the past hurts so I can get on with my life."

Marjorie didn't look as if she believed her. "As long as you're sure. My offer still stands. If you're having trouble meeting your bills…"

"You're a good friend, Marjorie. But I couldn't accept the help."

"Look, just because I'm an avid follower of the Stevens doesn't mean I'd expect information from you," she said, sounding hurt.

Kaitland sighed. "I know that. I guess I just have too much pride. Besides, all of the articles you've written about Max and Rand have been tongue-in-cheek. No one does humor better than you."

"Because I don't take them as seriously as other reporters do," Marjorie said, smiling. "Hey, they're celebrities, but they're human, too. They deserve some breaks sometimes."

"I never will forget the article you wrote when Rand's wife died. Highlighting the good, not wondering how he would survive another day blind or without his wife."

Marjorie blushed and then shrugged. "Enough about them. I did come by hoping you might be willing to drop a tidbit about what's going on. But my main reason was to find out if you're okay. I know you were hurt years ago by Max. You were devastated, actually. I was shocked when I realized you might be working for him again. I just wanted to make sure it wasn't a necessity."

What could Kaitland say? Yes, it was. She had to have the money. But she liked being around Max, too. Oddly, at the same time that it was a painful reminder of the one disastrous event in her life, it was also a comfort. "Don't worry, Marjorie."

"So, what about that lunch?" Marjorie asked, changing the subject. "Do you feel like getting away and just shooting the breeze like we used to do?"

Kaitland smiled. At one time, she and Marjorie had been very close. Over the years, they'd drifted apart and only got together occasionally. "Can I take a rain check on that? My car kaputed on me. I have to plug a leaking radiator and be back at the Stevens' house before dark to relieve—'' She caught herself just in time.

"Sure. No problem," Marjorie said. "I've been swamped and, to tell you the truth, I was on my way to an appointment but thought to put it off if you were available. I guess I was lucky to catch you home since you're living out there."

"Yeah, Marjorie. I'm living there. Now turn off that curiosity. If things weren't so touchy with Max I'd be glad to tell you more. I'm just afraid to risk it right now. Later, I promise to tell you all."

"How many times have I heard that in the past," Marjorie said, grinning. "Nope. I'll get my sources elsewhere, thank you very much. I'd never get the whole story out of you. You can't blame me for my curiosity, either. It comes with the job." Her expression turned sober. "You just be careful. I don't want to hear you've been hurt again. You're too good a friend."

Kaitland hugged her. "Thanks, Marjorie. Call me with a date when you're available. I'll try to get some time off."

She walked her friend to the door.

"Will do," Marjorie said.

She watched Marjorie leave, a soft smile on her face. Growing up together through all three schools had forged a bond between her and Marjorie. However, as much as she liked Marjorie, when she'd met Max, her relationship had cooled simply because Marjorie wrote the local stories that had to do with Max. Kaitland hoped one day Marjorie would get transferred to a different part of the paper and they could be close again.

Marjorie had once told her she loved the job but hated the strain it put on their relationship. And they usually did good, as long as nothing unusual was going on with the Stevens. Her editor insisted that stories about them sold papers, and tried to get them in as much as possible. So, Marjorie did the stories, or approved the stories, or bought the stories that had to do with Max or Rand.

Since her breakup with Max, it had been easier to go out to lunch with Marjorie. Still, now that she was working for Max, she worried about going out with her friend and Max hearing about it. It would be better if she and Max resolved what was between them first before she told him about Marjorie. He'd never met her. Marjorie had been on a leave of absence having a baby when she and Max had been dating. Since then Marjorie had lost her child and husband. She'd come back to work for the paper shortly after Max had broken their engagement.

And now she wasn't sure how to tell Max that one of her dear friends was a reporter. He'd just love that.

Oh, well. It was none of his business. She wouldn't say anything to hurt him, and Marjorie wouldn't use her friendship to approach Max. Things should be okay.

She went to the hall closest and grabbed her box of tools. The car had to be fixed or she'd be late to Max's. She'd learned a lot about fixing a car in the last year and a half. She could change the oil or tires. She knew how to check belts, work on the timing, change a fuel filter. One of the men at church was a mechanic and he sometimes came over and helped her. He'd even invited her over a few times when he was doing something new so she would have an idea how to do the job if she ever had to later on.

Joe was a swell guy. She thanked God for his help.

She pushed open the door and was surprised to see Max's sleek Mercedes pulling into the driveway. Why in the world would he be here? The look on his face as he climbed out of the car told her he was angry about something.

"Why didn't you tell me?" he demanded, coming toward her.

Uh-oh, she thought. She'd done something to upset him. She started toward her car with the tools. "Tell you what?" she asked, not sure she wanted to know.

"About your finances. You're going to lose the house if—"

"You had no right!" she accused, dropping the tools and swinging around on him. "I told you not to go snooping around."

Max didn't even have the decency to look abashed. "I was worried."

"Well, worry about someone else. I'm fine. As soon as my job is done with you, I'll be able to pay the taxes and the last of my grandmother's outstanding bills and be in the black again."

"But you shouldn't have to struggle—"

"Pu-leeeze!" she groaned. "Max. People struggle every day. I'm making it."

"Just look at what you're driving," he said.

"I knew you'd overreact if I told you," she grumbled. "And my car is just fine." She lifted the hood and started examining the radiator.

"If it's just fine, then what are you doing?"

She scowled. "My radiator is leaking. I'm going to plug it until I can get a new one installed. The plug will work for a while."

"You're going to... Since when do you know anything about cars, Katie?"

"Since I've had to learn," she replied sharply.

"Oh, Katie, che'rie," Max said, his voice filled with sadness.

"Don't you dare pity me!"

Max immediately wiped the sad look from his face. "That would be like a mouse taking pity on a lion and going into the cage so he could eat him. You have a bite in you when you're mad, Kaitland. One I don't remember being there before."

She shrugged. "As long as you remember it's here now."

Max slipped out of his casual jacket and rolled up his sleeves.

Kaitland stared as his muscular arms appeared inch by inch. He was so gorgeous, she thought dispiritedly. "What are you doing?"

"I'm gonna fix the car."

"Oh?" she asked, arching an eyebrow, her mind temporarily off those strong arms that he was revealing to her. "And you know how to fix a car?"

"Of course. I'm a man, aren't I?"

She glared. "That was sexist!"

He smiled smugly. "I know." Inching her aside, he began to poke around under the hood. "Actually, Rand and I went through a stage where we rebuilt cars. It was fun. We learned a lot."

"Well, I've learned a lot, too," she said defensively.

He lifted his head and stared at her in surprise. "Che'rie, I was only joking with you. Obviously you have learned a lot if you know your radiator is leaking and know how to plug it. Not many people ever learn more than how to tell the mechanic to change the oil."

A small smile lifted the corners of her mouth. "Well,

I did that at one time. But a friend at church has been giving me lessons on how to fix things on my car.''

"Good going, Katie. You've always been resourceful.''

A pall fell over the conversation as Katie realized how that could be applied to the past. Max went to work on the car, Kaitland helping him as he asked for tools or handed her something to hold.

"I'll change the oil while we're doing this," he said finally as he finished working on the radiator.

"Did it two weeks ago," she said.

"Very good." He wiped his hands on a cloth Kaitland handed him. "Why didn't your brother help you out?" he asked at last.

Kaitland sighed. "Why should he?" Kaitland explained how her grandmother had inexplicably cut her stepbrother out of her will and how he'd blamed Kaitland for it.

"That's no excuse," Max said. "I'd like to get my hands on him and have him try to hand me that rubbish," he said. "But right now, I want to take you out to dinner."

Kaitland stared, shocked. "Me?"

He rolled his eyes. "No one else is around. And I missed lunch."

"Oh, Max! Why didn't you tell me. I can fix you something—"

"I want to take you out to dinner, Katie. That was one of the reasons I came by."

Suspiciously, she asked, "This doesn't have anything to do with my finances, does it?"

Max scowled. "Don't mention that to me. I'm still mad over that. But no. I just thought it would be nice to go out for dinner, as…friends."

He sounded as if the word was hard to pronounce. But at least he was trying. "Just let me change," she said, deciding to go along.

"I'll finish this up and wait for you on the porch."

He watched Katie go and wondered how he was going to tell her this car was going to need a major overhaul if it was to keep running. It looked like a wreck waiting to happen. The idea that she was driving around in this, with the kids. It gave him cold chills. It might have been a decent car when she'd bought it, but it was just too old now. She was going to keep putting in more money repairing it than it was worth. He had taken a moment to examine the wiring and saw many frayed places in it. And that was only the beginning.

He sighed.

"So, it *is* you!"

Max hadn't heard the person approach. But he knew the voice. His eyes narrowing, he stepped back from the car. "Hello, Robert."

Robert, looking suspicious, glanced toward the house. "Just what are you doing over here, and to Kaitland's car?"

"Fixing it," Max said, his anger at the brother seeping out. "It's a shame Katie has to drive something like that when you drive a brand-new sports car. But then, I suppose you don't care that she is about to lose everything she owns."

Robert scowled. "What are you talking about? She's not about to lose everything. If she was, she would have told me."

"Robert!" Katie had just come out on the porch. Her eyes glanced back and forth between the two and she hurried down the steps. "I didn't know you were coming by."

"Yeah, well. If I'd known Don Juan was here, I wouldn't have."

Max knew it for the lie. Robert could have driven past if he hadn't wanted to see Kaitland while Max was around. "Did you tell your brother that you're in the red?" Max asked.

Kaitland gasped.

Robert looked at her. "He's lying, isn't he, Kaitland?"

Kaitland shot Max a furious look, then addressed her stepbrother. "You've been upset lately. I never got a chance to mention it. Besides, I knew you were estranged from Mimi and so I saw no reason to ask you to help pay her medical bills."

"Medicare should have covered them."

"It did most, plus her other insurance. And some of her money covered the rest."

"But cancer is a very expensive illness," Max added. "So, Kaitland had to sell her car, sell off stocks and bonds and now is working for me so she can earn enough money to pay the taxes on this house."

"I'll be fine once those are paid," Kaitland said. "You make me sound like a pauper. In a month or two my struggling will be over."

"Why didn't you come to me, Kaitland?" Robert demanded. "I might not have liked your grandmother, but I would have helped you out."

Max was surprised at the earnestness in his expression. But Robert ruined it when he added, "Anything would have been better than going back and working for him."

"Robert!" Kaitland admonished.

"Spoken like a true—"

"Max!" Kaitland warned him.

He sighed. "I am sorry, che'rie. But the fact is, your brother did not care enough to look out for you and it is upsetting."

Robert scowled at Max. "I will see to any other outstanding bills, Kaitland. You have my word on that. However, as for coming back and visiting you, you'll have to get rid of him first."

He stormed off.

Kaitland's shoulders slumped.

"I'm sorry, Kaitland. But why do you let him come by when he only hurts you?"

"You show a true Christian attitude, don't you, Max?" she said. "He's my brother. I would never turn him away, just like you'd never turn Rand away."

"But Rand and I get along."

"What if you didn't? Would you still turn him away."

Max opened his mouth to retort, then paused. "I have really wronged him, haven't I?" Max said ruefully. "I was so angry that he let you live like this, barely scraping by...this whole thing was my fault. Next time I see Robert, I'll be sure to apologize."

He reached out and caught her under the chin. When her eyes reluctantly met his, he said, "And I apologize to you now. You're right. It was very unchristian of me to react that way. I lowered myself. Please forgive me for hurting you, che'rie."

She shrugged. "Fine."

He grinned. "You're cute when you pout. But I guess it's better than you being truly angry and taking a swing."

The corner of her mouth quirked up.

"I would be laid out on the sidewalk, groaning in pain," he said, "and all of the people passing by would recognize me and call the papers and then I would end up on the front page with the headline that you had laid me low."

Both sides of her mouth quirked up, then she giggled. "You're ridiculous, do you know that?"

"I try, che'rie. It's worth it to see you smile. Now, let's go get some dinner."

She hesitated.

"I owe you at least that after the total jerk I made of myself."

She smiled. "Okay. But nothing expensive."

Chapter Ten

"I thought I said nothing expensive," she said, looking around at the steak house uneasily. She'd only been inside Ruth Chris's with Max before. She would never be able to afford it on what she made.

He shrugged. "I feel like a steak."

Kaitland looked at Max. His casual suit still made him look more elegant than any other man she knew. She wondered if Max knew what grunge was. Didn't he ever just pull on any old thing? She was exceedingly glad she'd put on her white sleeveless dress and pinned up her hair. She'd known this wouldn't be a fast-food date.

Looking around, she was grateful to see she didn't look out of place. She smiled at Max. "Well, I feel like seafood, if that's all right with you."

Max looked up and his eyes darkened, just like the old days, she thought, her heart suddenly tripping. "Whatever you want tonight is all right, che'rie."

The low drawl of his voice, combined with the dim lights and soft music, sent shivers up her spine.

The waitress chose that moment to arrive and take their orders. When she left, Max turned back to her. Reaching out, he touched her hand, casually stroking it. "I again want to apologize for my behavior tonight. It was inexcusable."

"Why do you dislike my brother so much?" she asked, trying to ignore the warmth of his hand on hers.

He smiled, though it was a tight smile that conveyed displeasure not uneasiness. "I've never mentioned this before, che'rie, but there are rumors that Robert plays dirty. No one has ever said anything specific, but still, it's hard to discount so many rumors. And an acquaintance of mine once mentioned, before he realized what he was saying, that your brother had ruined a man's career. He never went into details. But watching the way he treats you seems confirmation enough for me. It hurts me to see him use you."

"He's my brother. I can only hope one day he'll change."

"I know, che'rie. One day, with God's help, perhaps Robert will change."

The food arrived and the conversation lapsed as both tasted their entrées.

"Have you heard any more on the missing mother?" Kaitland asked, before taking another bite of her scampi.

Max shook his head. "I expect Dugan will find something any day. He likes to say he can find a mosquito in the middle of a desert."

Kaitland chuckled. "In a desert, huh?"

Max shrugged. "What can I say? He is from Texas. Their sayings are strange there."

"You have several stores in Texas," she said, surprised.

He grimaced. "And they all do wonderful business. The people are nice, but, as I said, they are very different from the people here."

She nodded. "If you say so. As I've never left Louisiana for more than a short vacation, I wouldn't know."

"You'll have to go with me sometime..."

Kaitland looked up.

Max cleared his throat.

"I meant to mention that everything went fine at the church," Kaitland said.

"What are you talking about?"

Kaitland blushed. "I thought Sarah told you. I'm...it's not important."

Max laid down his fork. "If you felt the need to bring up the subject, then it's important, Kaitland. What is it?"

She shrugged. "Jake called me. He was worried about the publicity. I told him everything was okay, but I was going to use the rest of my vacation, even if you find the mother first, simply because I didn't want the publicity to adversely affect the church."

"Jake asked you to take the time?" he demanded quietly.

"No!" Kaitland replied, horrified. "I didn't say that. I said, I insisted on taking the maximum vacation whether you found the kids' mother or not. Jake is a wonderful man. He has worked hard at building the church and he has just started on a major inner-city project. The way the media is, I was afraid they'd trace me to the day care and start hounding the church, trying to dig up anything they could. And not everyone on the committee is as understanding as Jake. Jake does his best to avoid controversy where his teachers and assistants are concerned. A few have even stepped down temporarily if anything questionable came up until all was cleared up. He's a good man and I don't want to see him hurt.''

He shook his head. "I understand and I'm sorry my thoughtlessness caused this problem.''

"No, Max,'' Kaitland said, reaching out and taking his hand. "It wasn't you. *It* was the paper.''

"But it caused you grief. No one likes that.''

She shrugged. "I suppose it happens and there's nothing we can do about it no matter how distasteful it is.''

His eyes darkened with what she thought was pain and then the expression was gone.

"Has Jake ever stepped down, I wonder?''

Kaitland shrugged again, her eyes not leaving his, very aware of how he held her hand and refused to release it. "I have no idea. Like I said, he's a good man.''

Suddenly she stiffened.

Max saw her face pale, before she pasted on a serene smile and stared him in the eyes. But the Kaitland he knew was gone. Her eyes were blank, lifeless. "What is—'' He stopped as he was interrupted from behind.

"Max Stevens. I thought that was you. It's been simply ages since I've seen you. Where have you been keeping yourself?''

Max looked up to see Winna Richardson and her husband, the senator, standing by his side. He felt Kaitland's hand become clammy and her gentle tug.

He released her fingers and stood. Kissing Winna's hand, he smiled. "I've been so busy with the store, dear lady, that I've had no time for other pursuits.''

She laughed. "Well, we're having a party in two

weeks. I'll be sure to send you an invitation. And who is this?''

She turned to Kaitland. That serene smile was still there, but Kaitland looked as though one wrong word would crack her emotions wide open.

He introduced her and both Winna and the senator shook her hand.

"Ah, yes," Winna said. "I've met you before. Your brother attends a lot of the charity functions, does he not?''

"Yes. Yes, he does," Kaitland replied.

The senator's wife turned back to Max. "Bring her along if you'd like. We'd love to have her." She winked.

The senator nodded, and then both strolled away.

Max resumed his seat. Kaitland looked green around the gills. She placed her napkin by her plate but didn't look up.

Max tossed his napkin onto the table. Guilt was written all over her. How could she have done *that* with the senator? A senator who was married? He couldn't believe his Katie was that type of person. Why? Why? Why?

He motioned for the check. "I'll drop you off to pick up your car." He had no intention of bringing up the painful subject. But he couldn't miss the relief in her posture when he avoided it.

He paid the bill, escorted her to the car and drove her home. Not a word passed between them.

"I'll see you in a little bit," he said just before driving off.

"Father, I can't stand this," Max said as he drove home. "At one time, I thought not knowing was the best route. It hurt too much. But now...I just don't

know. It hurts too much to think about it. Katie looked
so defeated, so guilty and I just can't understand why.
If she had planned her liaison with the senator on pur-
pose, she wouldn't look that way. But what other reason was there? She is not the type to casually fall into
someone's arms. She's always been quiet, serene, careful. Of course, once you get to know her, she's not the
same person. But she wouldn't do something like
that…except for those pictures.

"Please help me. Help her. No, help *us*. I can't do
it. I need Your help, Your guidance. Because without
You, I've already made a mess. I think I'm beginning
to agree with Kaitland. I only want the pain gone so
we can go on with our lives."

Then, because no one else could see him, he allowed
the tortured expression to show on his face. "Your will
be done in this."

Peace flooded him and he realized that by letting go
and allowing God to take care of the problem, a tre-
mendous weight lifted from his shoulders. True, the
problems weren't solved, but he knew, with a certainty,
that the solution would be forthcoming.

Chapter Eleven

"I was sorry to hear about your grandmother."

They were at dinner. Kaitland had one child on each side of her, while Max sat next to Maddie. Elizabeth was across from her and Rand next to Elizabeth. She smiled at Rand's words. "I got the flowers. Thank you. She was a Christian so it makes it easier, even though I do miss her."

"It gets easier as time goes by."

Kaitland knew he was speaking from experience.

Elizabeth reached over and placed her hand gently on Rand's arm.

He smiled and dished up some asparagus then passed the platter to Max.

"Tell us about the trip," Max said, taking the asparagus and avoiding the grip of the little girl, who protested loudly. Max passed the vegetables on, then speared one of the green stalks from his plate and handed it to Maddie, who promptly quieted and began chewing on it.

Rand gaped. Kaitland smiled at his expression, but

covered it by wiping her mouth with her napkin. Bobby, clearly feeling left out, pounded on his tray. Kaitland stabbed a piece of baked chicken and held it up to Bobby. He wanted none of this fork business— as usual—and peeled the chicken from the fork then popped it in his mouth. Kaitland was careful to keep a watchful eye on the children as she fed them tidbits while Rand talked about his trip.

She also noted that Max did his share of feeding Maddie. She wondered if he realized how attached he was becoming to the children.

"Want!" Maddie interrupted, reaching for Max's plate.

Max smiled, patted Maddie's hand, waiting to see to her as Rand continued talking about the island he and Elizabeth had visited.

"Want!" Maddie demanded again.

Kaitland saw the stubborn look on her face. Maddie was getting ready for a tantrum. In the weeks she'd been here, Kaitland had come to recognize that look.

"Max," she interrupted.

He looked around just as Maddie tossed her plate.

It hit him in the chest. "Oh, no!"

Kaitland started to stand.

Max waved her down. "I'm getting used to this." Turning to Maddie, he gave her a stern look. "No, no. Maddie, bad. You don't throw your food." Then his face softened. "But Max was bad, too. I shouldn't have ignored you." With amazement, all three watched Max fix another plate, make sure it was suctioned down to the tray this time and then give the child another stalk of asparagus.

"You're going to ruin your reputation if you let any-one see you this way," Rand finally drawled.

"What?" Max asked.

"The fun-loving bachelor. People are going to worry if they see you like this."

Max looked to where he had gotten distracted with Maddie, then to his spoiled shirt, and an embarrassed smile crossed his face. "Well, you know how rumors are."

"Yeah, I do," Rand said, though he was grinning as if he was reveling in the scene.

Kaitland enjoyed their banter, but with a bittersweet ache. The more Max played with the kids, the more she realized what she'd missed out on with this man.

"Well, it sounds like you had a wonderful time, but I think these little ones need a bath," Max said.

Rand laughed.

Max sighed. "Two kids takes more than one set of hands. Darlene has the night off tonight. Katie will need help. So, just get used to seeing me helping around here the next few weeks, Rand, unless you want to help her," Max added defensively.

Rand lifted his hands, but didn't stop laughing.

Elizabeth socked him in the arm. "You've been laughing at the situation ever since we returned. Cut your brother some slack."

"I am. I am. I think it's very good training for when he's an uncle." He patted Elizabeth's still-flat tummy. "Go on. Go give them a bath."

Kaitland stood. "Let me take Maddie. She's the messiest."

Max lifted Bobby into his arms and Kaitland turned toward the stairs. "Are you ready for a bath, buddy?" she heard Max ask.

Rand suddenly broke into more gales of laughter.

Even Elizabeth chuckled.

Kaitland turned to see what was the matter. "Again?" she asked, dismayed, seeing the stain spread down Max's shirt.

"Again?" Rand asked, his eyebrows shooting up.

"We'll have no trouble potty training this one," Max said to his brother. "Just put one of my shirts over the potty-chair and he'll do it every time."

Mortified, Kaitland hurried over to Max. "I'm so sorry, Max. Why don't I just give them a bath tonight? I appreciate your offer, but you don't have to..."

"I want to," Max said, his gaze reassuring her. Then with a rueful smile, he added, "Besides, I'm already a mess."

They walked up the stairs together. Kaitland could easily imagine them as a family taking their children to bed. Realizing how dangerous those thoughts were, she instead asked Max, "Are you sure you want to do this?"

Max smiled. "Believe it or not, I'm having fun." His smile faded. "I've been restless lately, bored with life. Like I was missing something. These children have filled a void I didn't know existed. I need to get out more, do more charity work, get in touch with people, I suppose. But because of the publicity the family attracts, I tend to isolate myself."

Kaitland didn't comment. Max was looking at these kids as more than charity, she was afraid. He truly enjoyed them. She knew, from being a foster mother in the past, that you could easily grow to love the kids in your care only to have your heart ripped out when it was time for them to leave. But she also knew she wouldn't trade that experience for anything in the world. She wasn't married, would probably never marry, so the only kids she would ever have would be those who passed through her doors from Social Services.

"If you'll watch them while I prepare the bathroom?" Kaitland asked.

"No problem," Max said, and sat down in a chair. The two children, released, began to squeal and run around the room. Maddie, of course, danced back and forth in her exuberance. Bobby quickly made his way to the toy box where he collapsed and began to play.

Kaitland laid out the towels on the floor and along the rim of the tub. She ran just enough water to fill the bottom of the tub, then went to get the children.

Max was on the floor making childish faces at Maddie, who was suspended over his head. When he saw Kaitland, he immediately stopped. "She was bored. I had to find something to do." Scooping up one child under each arm, he started toward the bathroom.

Horrified, Kaitland took Bobby.

Max chuckled. "Don't worry. These two, I have decided, are indestructible."

He looked around in approval at the bathroom. "I take it they must make quite a mess."

"It's an experience," Kaitland replied as she stripped down Bobby.

Max removed Maddie's clothes and put her in the tub. "Wheee!" she cried out and splashed.

Max blinked as water splashed him in the face. "A definite experience."

Before Kaitland knew what he was up to, he had snagged the bottom of his shirt and lifted it off. "I'm going to need a whole new wardrobe of things that aren't *dry-clean only*. That, or buy up a line of dry-cleaning stores."

Kaitland didn't comment. She couldn't.

She'd forgotten how beautiful Max was. That was one of the reasons she'd always enjoyed swimming with him. His body was a work of art. She could sit back and appreciate how well in shape he kept himself. Hair was sprinkled across his tanned chest and narrowed down to his pants. She had thought one day to be able to claim that body as hers, too. She'd always been dowdy-looking, as far as she was concerned, and it had flattered her outrageously that such a beautiful man found her beautiful, too, wanted her as his wife, loved her and was willing to promise to be hers for the rest of his life. Tears pricked her eyes.

She swallowed and turned her attention to Bobby.

Max's strong, tanned hands joined hers in the tub as they bathed both children in silence. Finally, Max said, "I can't understand why the mother deserted her children."

"Who knows," Kaitland replied, soaping Bobby's arms as he splashed and gurgled. "As you pointed out to me earlier, there are any number of reasons. You're rich. You could give them a better home. Or maybe she just couldn't take care of them."

"I'd find a way for these two little cherubs."

"Maybe this was her way," Kaitland said. Turning her gaze to his, she continued earnestly, "She's got to know you and know what type of person you are or she wouldn't have named one of her babies after you. Maybe she knew you were kind and gentle." Her gaze slid away, focusing on the children once again. "I know that's why my mother left my stepbrother and me in my grandmother's care."

"You never talked about her with me—before," Max said quietly.

"Maybe I was caught up in the romance of dating

the Max Stevens," she replied. "I don't know. I do know that my grandmother was a sweet but stern lady who loved Robert and me very much."

"Did you ever...did you miss your parents much?" Max continued questioning as Maddie slowly relaxed in the tub and let Max bathe her.

"I suppose I did. But whereas Robert ran hard, using alcohol and women to fill that void, I ran to God. God gave me a peace and acceptance I needed. I found out He could be a comforter when my grandmother didn't understand what I was going through."

She lifted Bobby into her arms and wrapped him in a huge, fluffy, peach terry-cloth towel.

"And despite that, you still talk with Robert." He sounded amazed and just a little humbled, but couldn't help it. Kaitland had such a forgiving heart. More so than anyone he knew.

Holding Maddie, Max followed her into the next room. He chucked Maddie under the chin before grabbing a diaper and watching Kaitland skillfully wrap it around the child.

"He's my brother. I'd never stop talking to him. I do pray for him though. I keep hoping he'll come back to God, turn away from the life he's leading."

"All you can do is trust God and pray," he agreed. Taking the sleeper that Kaitland had laid out, he tried to get Maddie's feet into it. Just as he'd get one in and start on the other, the little termagant would pull out the first foot then wiggle her toes.

"Here, let me dress Maddie," Kaitland said. "You finish up Bobby."

Max realized Bobby was almost asleep. Without arguing, he brushed past her and worked Bobby's feet into the sleeper. He noted Kaitland had put the sleeves on first. A much more effective way, he was sure. Snapping up the garment, he carefully lifted the sleeping child into his arms.

Bobby only stirred a bit. Tenderly, he brushed a lock of hair off Bobby's forehead. "They're so small, so innocent. I hate to see a strike against them already."

"What do you mean?" Kaitland asked, taking Maddie to the rocking chair where she sat and began to rock her.

Max sat on the edge of the bed and watched Kaitland, thinking how beautiful she looked sitting there, how maternal. Even as he had the thought he realized that he had a child on his shoulder and that he was patting the boy's back. He wondered how he looked to Kaitland. "I wonder if the mother realizes these children will have to go into foster care if she doesn't come back."

"Who knows what was on her mind. Maybe she thought you'd just keep them."

He laughed, though it sounded unsteady. "Keep them? I'm not a father. I could never be a father. I mean, there's more to being a father than this."

Isn't there? he asked himself. You had to be married and wait nine months while you read scores of books on the subject and then you had to go through the labor and delivery and they would have a mother and you missed many nights of sleep...or at least, that's what he'd always thought being a parent meant.

"I wonder if, when I find the kids' mother, she'll agree to let the children be adopted out to someone. I'd be more than willing to contact a lawyer and arrange everything."

Kaitland glanced up at him. "I'm sure she'd want that. Max, she wouldn't have left them if she could've kept them. I know people do that all the time, but look at the diaper bags, and the clothes. Whoever was their mother cared for these children deeply. She only wants what's best. When you find her, I'm sure she'll thank you for your help.''

Kaitland stood and quietly glided across the floor to the cribs. She lay down Maddie. Leaning over, she placed a kiss on the little girl's cheek. "Good night, sweet one." Then she said a soft prayer over the child.

Turning, she held out her arms for Bobby. Max stood and handed her the child then stepped back and watched while she did the same with Bobby.

Max stepped forward, and for the first time, placed a kiss on Maddie's cheek. It was soft and warm. A shuddering little sigh escaped her mouth and she popped her thumb in it. The he turned to Bobby, placed a kiss on his cheek—he was already sucking his thumb. Turning to Kaitland, he intended to tell her good-night. But when he saw her quickly glance at his chest, then avert her gaze, he forgot his intentions. When he'd stripped off his shirt, he hadn't thought about Kaitland being in the room. How many times had they gone swimming together? He didn't realize Kaitland would even notice.

The longing he'd seen so briefly in her eyes—he realized it mirrored what was in his own heart. Before he could think better of it, he stepped forward and took Kaitland in his arms. "Good night, Katie," he whispered huskily, and then, lowering his head, he touched his lips to hers, a gentle kiss, nondemanding, but exquisitely tender, and filled with longing.

The kiss brought back good memories. Too many. And with one last gentle kiss, he lifted his head.

Staring down at her soft features his heart twisted

with remorse. *Why? Oh, Katie, why?* his anguish cried
out.

Dropping his arms, he turned and left the room.

Katie opened her eyes, saw Max scoop up his discarded shirt and leave without another word. Gently,
she touched her lips, shaking with old desires she'd
forgotten existed.

How could she have forgotten how much she'd enjoyed kissing Max, how sweet and tender his embraces
were? Trembling from head to toe, she sank onto the
edge of the rocker.

She wondered if Max had forgotten, too.

Or was that why he'd left in such a hurry?

With a sigh she remembered other times she and
Max had shared a tender kiss or look of longing and
wondered if Max recalled them. But more important,
she wondered what he would do tomorrow after what
had just happened tonight.

Would he acknowledge the feelings still between
them or pretend that nothing at all had happened?

Kaitland wasn't sure she wanted to know.

Chapter Twelve

He did neither. He completely avoided her. It had been five days since the kiss they'd shared and she hadn't seen Max. She knew he'd been in to visit the children. Darlene had told her that. Evidently, he was scoping out her schedule and working around it.

She'd explained to him once before that the children needed him in their life. Well, she needed him too…at least occasionally. True, she was an employee, but that kiss changed things.

You didn't kiss your employees. At least, that was the excuse she was using concerning Max.

Both Rand and Elizabeth were giving her strange looks. She figured they blamed her for Max's absences from meals and the odd hours he now stayed at work. She knew Max blamed her for that accidental kiss or he wouldn't be avoiding her. And she didn't want him avoiding her because she wouldn't get the problems between them solved if he kept hiding out.

Therefore, now that the kids were taking their morning nap, she was going to hunt down Max and try talk-

ing to him. She'd come up with the perfect excuse—
the children needed to get out and she wanted to make
sure it was okay to take them on an all-day excursion.

Of course, she shouldn't take that kind of trip with
them without making sure it was okay with Max. She
never took them off the property without letting him
know since there were always reporters hounding his
steps.

She checked her hair in the mirror, to see if her
French braid was neat. Her jeans and soft baby blue
top brought out the green of her eyes and the blush...
Realizing she was checking her appearance for his
sake, she rolled her eyes. If she went down there looking as if she'd dressed ready to kill, he'd run even
farther away. She only wanted to set things straight,
get back on an even keel, not chase him off.

She went downstairs, checking room by room as she
passed them. In one room she stumbled onto Rand and
Elizabeth hugging.

"Oh!" Her cheeks pinkened. "I'm sorry." She
started to back out, embarrassed to catch them in an
intimate embrace.

Rand grinned, but didn't release his wife. "Honeymoon, you know. What do you need?"

He looked so much like Max it made her remember
Max's embrace. "I was just looking for Max."

"The study."

She nodded and backed out.

"Close the door, please, Kaitland."

She heard a muttered exclamation from Elizabeth,
but didn't stop to hear what Elizabeth was berating
Rand for. Rand's husky laugh followed her out the
door.

She didn't remember Rand ever being this carefree

five years ago. He'd always been at the office when she'd visited before. Rarely had she seen him around the house. Come to think of it, he was *very* carefree, laughing, joking, his eyes twinkling with a merriment she'd never seen in him, but often seen in Max.

Except that she never saw it in Max now, only occasionally, when one of the children did something to amuse him.

Going to the study, she found him there. He was sitting with his back to the door, holding something in his hand and staring out the balcony doors. "Excuse me, Max, but I had heard you were home and…"

Max whirled, his eyes widening in surprise. Quickly, he slid a paper under a manila envelope on his desk. "What can I do for you, Katie?"

Curious, she eyed his desk. She watched him nonchalantly fold his hands over the envelope.

"Look, Max, I know you've been avoiding me and we need to talk."

She hadn't been going to say that at all. She wanted to call the words back, start out softer instead. But it was too late and Max reacted the way she thought he would.

He sighed, a look of pained frustration on his face. "It was a mistake. I was feeling close to the kids, enjoying the intimacy they offered, and I stepped over the line. I shouldn't have. I hope we can just forget it."

She shouldn't be hurt by his attitude, knowing it was purely defensive on his part, but she was. "Forget it? Well, now, Max, that's going to be pretty hard to do unless you tell me you go around kissing all your female employees like that."

She waited. When he didn't answer, her anger at his

continued rejection made her fist her hands on her hips. She was bursting over everything that was between them. All she wanted was peace again. Was that so much to ask?

Max blew out a breath. Shoving himself up from the desk, he went to the balcony doors and resumed staring out. "It doesn't matter what I do with *all my female employees,*" Max replied sarcastically. "You and I are no longer dating."

Kaitland reeled as if she'd been slapped. But instead of retreating, she went forward. "I was out of line," she said quietly. "You're right. But, Max, I'm working in this house. You can't wash hot and cold like this. If we're going to work together, then we need to establish some ground rules, forget the past and go on from here."

She was by his desk now. She absently glanced down to what he had hidden, wondering what it was. Kaitland would like to think, under normal circumstances, she wouldn't have looked. But when she saw a corner of the picture that showed a bed, a man and a woman's leg…a sick feeling rose inside her. Surely it couldn't be, not after all this time.

She reached down and pulled the picture out from under the envelope. Cold sweat broke out on her.

"No, Katie. Don't look."

She and the senator. The senator pinning her to the bed as he kissed her. Her dress hiked up to her thighs with his leg wedged between hers.

She was going to be sick.

Across the bottom was scrawled the word *Remember.*

"Oh, Max," she whispered, tears coming to her

eyes. After all these years, she would have hoped he'd at least forgiven her her part in the whole mess.

"Listen to me, Katie," Max said, coming toward her, but her eyes were so full of tears she couldn't see what he was feeling, could only hear desperation in his voice. The desperation of someone guilty, caught in his crime.

The picture slid from her fingers, and without another word, she turned and fled.

"Katie! Katie, come back here now!" Max ran after her, but stopped at the door, watching as she raced up the stairs. "Katie!" he called out, anger in his voice.

The door down the hall flew open and Rand came out. Seeing Katie's flight, he turned on his brother. He strode angrily toward Max. But as he watched Max, anger slowly left his face until concern was left. "I was about to blast you for upsetting her again, until I saw your face, little brother. Want to talk?"

Miserable, Max nodded. "I thought maybe she had something to do with it. But I don't think so now. I should have made sure it was put up..."

"What are you talking about, Max?"

"Close the door, will you?"

Rand pushed the door closed. "Now, will you explain why you scared ten years off Elizabeth's life and left Katie in tears...again?"

"You've always blamed me for our breakup, haven't you, Rand?"

Rand sighed. "I don't blame you. I think you should have talked with her, tried to work things out. It was obvious the way you grieved that you loved her, Max. I don't understand why she would do something like that, but maybe she was being blackmailed, or she had to have money. I don't know. But you never gave her a chance to explain.''

''That's just it. She had a month to tell me, but never did.''

Rand sat down by Max on the couch, staring off in the distance. ''I know that. And I've always really liked Kaitland. That's why I can't understand what happened. She just wasn't that type of girl.'' He sighed. ''I wish it could have worked out. But, it didn't. And no one's to blame if you choose to go separate ways. But if that's the case and she's now tormenting you so, why do you keep her here?''

''This has nothing to do with my feelings for Katie.'' Max stood and went to his desk. He brought back the picture and handed it to Rand.

Rand took one look at it and started to discard it, then paused. ''Where'd you get this?''

''At least *you* believe I haven't been tormenting myself with old pictures of Katie. This was in today's mail.''

Rand frowned, sitting forward. ''Why?''

''My question exactly. When it happened five years ago I could understand why. Someone was warning me about what was going on behind my back. But why now? Katie and I aren't involved. These pictures are old. I know all about her.''

''Unless someone is worried you'll become involved with her again.''

''But why would it matter? The only thing I can come up with is that Katie is somehow involved and it's the precursor to getting blackmail money.''

''You think whoever was trying to blackmail you five years ago has come back?''

Max shrugged.

"And you think Katie is involved."

"It seems strange that when she shows up, the pictures suddenly show up again." He handed Rand an envelope with two more pictures inside.

"Katie saw these and thinks you kept them around to remind you of her betrayal."

Max nodded. "And I started to go after her. But now I'm not so sure if I should. I'm tempted to try and mend the fences, Rand. I'd like to date her again. But these pictures, it brings it all back. I don't see how we'll ever be able to let go of the past."

Rand was quiet a long time. "You're going to have to forgive her, Max."

"I have forgiven her," Max argued, appalled.

"Have you forgiven yourself, too, then?"

"What do you mean?"

"I know you. You blame yourself for her going to someone else. I saw it in your eyes right after it happened." Rand's voice dropped, more emotion than he usually showed sounding in every word he spoke as he stared Max in the eye. "And no matter how much you say you've forgiven her, you haven't. You may convince everyone else, but you won't even listen to an explanation from her. Why?"

Max turned from Rand's stare but wouldn't answer.

"Because you're afraid of what you might hear?" Rand asked.

Max scowled. "I don't want to hear that I wasn't what she needed. Call me vain, but I loved her. I can't face that."

"You're not vain, just hurting. Go to God, Max. Let Him heal your heart so you and Kaitland can both be healed. Even if you don't end up together, you need to go on, let go of this pain."

"But someone isn't going to let us, are they?" he said, motioning to the picture.

Rand slipped the picture into the folder and turned back to Max. "I'll get these to one of our lawyers. It's time someone else knew about this, so don't argue. We'll take it one day at a time. Don't tell Katie, if that's what you feel like. I won't interfere, but we have to consider that someone out there hasn't forgotten. This isn't some whim like we thought five years ago. Whoever wanted to blackmail us before is making it clear they're going to try again."

Max dropped his head back on the sofa. "I'm really sorry, Rand. This isn't much of a thing to come back to after your honeymoon."

Rand grinned. "I hate to tell you, brother, but the honeymoon ain't gonna end just because we have a few fiery trials to face. God will see us through, and Elizabeth isn't as worried about her reputation as Carolyn was. She's a real trouper and will thumb her nose at the media if this leaks out."

Max smiled, though he knew the expression looked weary. "I only hope Katie will be able to do the same, since these pictures are of her."

"Kaitland? It's me, Elizabeth. Can I come in?"

Kaitland quickly wiped the tears from her face before opening the bathroom door. "Are the children awake?"

Elizabeth rolled her eyes. "Do you really think I'm going to be distracted that easily? You know why I've come here. Rand and I almost had a cow when Max shouted downstairs. He never shouts. His voice just gets low and his eyes narrow when he's angry."

"Not this time."

"I know a woman in distress when I see one. That's why I came up to check on you when I saw you tear up the stairs."

Kaitland felt tears coming again. "Thank you, but there's nothing you can do."

Elizabeth grabbed her arm and dragged her over to the sofa. "Usually with my patients I tell jokes. Wanna hear one?"

"I don't think I'm exactly in a mood for a joke," she replied, the tears still sounding obvious in her voice.

"Then that's just the time you need it," Elizabeth said, then, "So, how many Stevens brothers does it take to screw in a lightbulb?"

Kaitland shook her head. "I don't know. Two?"

Elizabeth smiled. "Are you kidding? They're too thickheaded to realize they can do it themselves. They get a servant to do it."

Kaitland did smile. "That's awful."

"Well, those men can be pretty awful sometimes, too. I swear, there are times I'd like to hit Rand with a two-by-four...several times."

Kaitland laughed. "I know. Max is so stubborn. I thought he'd forgotten..." Her voice trailed off.

"What?"

Kaitland sighed. "You know Max and I were engaged to be married. It was a great time. We were so in love. I admit I was naive, a little awed by all of this." She swept her hand around the room. "Even my brother tried to convince me I wasn't in love with Max. But I was, very in love, despite how shy I was over the media attention and Max's money. And I thought he was in love with me."

She sighed again, her shoulders sagging as she remembered.

"My brother is a user," Kaitland continued. "Actually, he isn't really my brother. He's my stepbrother, as he will point out, but to me he's flesh and blood. When we were small, my mom married his dad. They died in an auto accident not too long afterward. We had nowhere to go, so my grandmother raised us both. Robert always felt like the outsider, claiming he didn't belong."

"And you felt guilty for that," Elizabeth concluded.

"Just a little. I love him. He had no family left after our parents died...except me. And he and my grandmother didn't get along. Anyway, he's gotten involved in lobbying and attends huge balls and fancy dinners. I'm very uncomfortable at these functions...you aren't going to discuss this with anyone, are you?" she suddenly asked, wringing her hands.

"Of course not!" Elizabeth said. "What you say won't leave this room. Gossip is a very distasteful thing."

Kaitland felt the trembling start deep down in her soul as she began to explain.

"I went to a party one night that my brother begged me to attend. During the party I got a note. I thought it was from Robert, asking me to meet him in his room. So, I went up there. Instead, a drunk senator was waiting. He—" Kaitland's eyes dropped. "He tried to rape me."

"Oh, dear." Elizabeth moved closer.

Kaitland felt her slip her arm around her and she gratefully leaned into the silent support Elizabeth offered.

"Rand's going to kill me for upsetting you."

"I'll handle Rand. If he kicks up a fuss, I'll just faint in his arms."

Despite the seriousness of the situation, Kaitland giggled. "You really are awful."

"I know. But don't you just love me."

Kaitland giggled again.

"So, what did Max say when you told him?"

"I didn't."

"You didn't tell Max?" She sounded incredulous.

"I was so embarrassed and ashamed. How could I look my fiancé in the eyes and tell him that at the party I'd gone to with my brother, a party, I might add, that Max had asked me not to go to with my brother because he believed Robert was only using me." She shuddered. "Anyway, how could I tell him that while there I met a man in my room and he was drunk and almost raped me."

"He needed to know."

Kaitland pulled away. "You're telling me. I kept wanting to tell him. Things became strained. I was awful. I pulled away from him whenever he hugged or kissed me. I couldn't deal with being touched. It wasn't Max. I needed him, but felt suffocated. It's hard to explain." She shuddered at the memories. "I also couldn't handle the hurt and confusion in Max's eyes, either. It killed me that whenever he would try to kiss me, I would stiffen up, only for him to pull back, and with such a look of hurt and confusion in his eyes. How could I explain what I felt?

"Just before the wedding, I decided to tell him. You see, it wasn't fair to Max. And I wanted to go to counseling and I didn't want to hide that from Max. Besides, I had decided I could trust him, that he wouldn't turn away in betrayal or disgust. After all, look what he'd been through the month after the incident, and he was still there despite how shabbily I had treated him.''

"What happened?" Elizabeth asked softly, taking Kaitland's hand. Kaitland noted her knuckles were white where she gripped them together.

What had she done? she mused. "He walked into the room where I was sitting and dropped some photographs in my lap. They were photos of me and the senator, lying on the bed in what looked like a very intimate embrace.

"Max knew which party they'd been taken at since I hadn't attended any others," she continued. "He made an unimportant comment inferring my betrayal. Then he turned around and walked out."

"Oh, Kaitland." Elizabeth's voice ached with remorse.

"That was five years ago. I thought it would be good to see him again, work through the past so we could get on with our lives. I even thought God was leading me here. But now I'm not so sure. Just now, when I went down to his study, he had one of the pictures, he was looking at it, and across the bottom was the word *Remember*."

"Oh, Kaitland," Elizabeth murmured again.

"I don't know what to do." Kaitland allowed the tears to flow again, crying out all her hurt and pain. Elizabeth murmured soft words of comfort as she held Kaitland.

"You know," Elizabeth said when Kaitland finished crying and pulled away. "Sometimes healing can be very painful. And a lot of times it doesn't happen overnight. We have to take it one day at a time. The blind patients I work with have to relearn the layout of their houses, the way to dress, to eat, to converse, everything. Our spiritual healings are like that, too. We have to take one day at a time and let God pull out each fear and pain and deal with it. That's one of the most painful processes you can go through, especially if the wound has set for very long. Like a broken bone that has to be rebroken and set, we sometimes have to have everything dredged up and the air cleared before the trust can be reestablished.''

Elizabeth handed her several tissues. "I guess what I'm saying is, if you think God sent you here, then play like a bulldog and clamp those teeth into this and don't let go, no matter how rough the ride. Keep smiling no matter how painful and let God do His work. I'll be praying for you and I know Rand will. He really likes you a lot. And, believe it or not, I bet Max is praying about this, too. Trust God to do His work, Kaitland. And trust Him to work it out for what's best for both you and Max.''

Kaitland leaned over and hugged Elizabeth. "Thanks, Elizabeth. You're right. I will." She stood. "Now, you'd better find Rand before he comes to make sure you're resting.''

Elizabeth groaned.

Kaitland chuckled. "And I'm going to go check on the kiddos. It's about time for them to get up. And every time I've been late getting them from Darlene, I've caught at least one of them eating something that's not edible!''

"I wish I could help," Elizabeth said, grinning.

"No you don't. You want to be with your husband. Now go.''

She watched Elizabeth leave. Her smile left her face as soon as Elizabeth was out of sight. Elizabeth was right. She had to trust God to handle the mess she'd made five years ago. And no matter what, she just had to grin and bear it and know God would work it out for the best.

Father, I'm leaving this in Your hands. My heart. Max's heart. Our future. Please handle this as You see fit and give me the courage to face Your answers.

As if on cue, one of the children could be heard from down the hall. *Thank You,* she added to the end of her prayer, then headed out of the room. Time to get back to doing what she was hired to do and just let God handle the rest.

Chapter Thirteen

Crash!

Max jumped up from the chair in his study. Tossing down the papers he'd been working on he hurried around the desk and to the door. He skidded to a stop just outside, staring in dismay at the scene before him.

He should have known not to come out here. Something had warned him. Kaitland was in a red bathing suit, holding both kids, who were wearing blue suits, with a broken vase scattered around her. And of course she wasn't wearing any shoes.

"I didn't mean to disturb you. Could you, um, possibly call for Sarah and we'll wait here?"

Max thought about doing exactly that. He hadn't wanted to be involved with Kaitland. He had decided to treat her as an employer would an employee and be courteous. He had figured that would set everything to right and they could go on. But seeing her here, like this... She was so vulnerable. Enough was enough. Rand was right. He should put forth the effort to be a friend. He walked forward. "Let me take the kids."

"No. Really. That's okay."

"Katie. Don't argue." Bobby came willingly and Maddie lunged. He took them across the floor, handing them to the butler who had just rounded the corner, and who immediately gaped like a fish out of water. Max grinned when he saw Bobby pull his wet fingers out of his mouth and rub them on Timms's shirt.

When he turned back to Kaitland, she was still standing in the same place staring in dismay at the mess around her. Smiling, he decided to enjoy her discomfort, only for a moment. After all, it had been he who had been miserable this last week. And maybe his sense of humor would restore her good mood. He hated seeing the cautious look in her eyes whenever he was around.

"Well, are you going to send for Sarah?" she asked.

"I don't know. What will you give me if I do?"

Kaitland glanced up, unsure.

He was happy when he saw her features relax. "I'll break some more stuff trying to climb up this table to get around these pieces of pottery if you don't," she retorted, placing her hands on her hips.

"You'd ruin my house?" he asked, feigning astonishment

"I don't see that I'd have any choice, Mr. Stevens."

"You could ask me for help," he replied smugly.

"I thought I did that."

"No, you wanted Sarah's help. How about asking me specifically?"

She crossed her arms.

He sighed. "Well, I suppose I'll have to help you anyway. So, where were you headed, the pool?"

"How'd you guess?" she replied sarcastically.

He came forward, pottery crunching under his feet. "I had a feeling."

Wary again, she watched his approach. "What are you doing?"

"Helping you out." He scooped her up. "You've lost weight," he commented.

She hit him on the shoulder. "That's none of your business. Now put me down!"

"I dunno." He lifted her, bouncing her slightly in his arms. "I might want to find out why you've gotten so skinny first."

"Max," she warned.

He grinned, carried her over to where the kids were and allowed her to slide down out of his arms. He saw that her cheeks were pink. The old heat warmed his body as he realized how much this woman still meant to him. Why *not* try to be friends? If that was all she wanted, surely he could work his way toward that.

"You're not going in alone with both of the kids, are you?" he suddenly asked, not seeing Darlene around.

"Of course I am. I'm a good swimmer."

"But I know these two," Max said, and making a sudden decision, added, "Go on, I'll be out in a minute."

"No! I mean, that's okay."

"Nonsense," Max replied, already heading up the stairs. "I was only doing the boring fiscal reports. Rand is back so my workload is much lighter, but I still need a break."

In minutes Max joined them at the pool, dressed in a pair of green and black bathing trunks. Kaitland watched him dive in and swim toward them. Maddie and Bobby were both in life preservers, having a blast.

"Catch, Maddie," Kaitland called. She tossed a small floating ball to Maddie.

Maddie squealed and reached out for it. Grabbing the ball, she threw it, and caught Max in the middle of the chest just as he surfaced. "Whoa, che'rie," Max drawled, fumbling and finally grabbing the hand-size ball.

"Mine!" Maddie demanded, holding out her hands.

Max chuckled and threw her the ball. Maddie threw the ball aside and held out her arms again. "Mine!"

"I think she means you," Kaitland said.

Max smiled. "Indeed she does." He moved forward and bussed Maddie on the cheek. Waving her arms wildly, she threw up water, squealing again.

Bobby blinked, shook his head from the drenching and then held out his arms, too. Kaitland intercepted Bobby, holding out her fingers and letting him pull himself along through the water. He was enraptured with the game, kicking his feet, laughing, shaking his head whenever he accidentally splashed water in his face.

All in all, it was a wonderful time of fun. "I told Sarah we'll have lunch out here," Max told her when he saw Darlene bringing food out to the table.

Kaitland was surprised. Not only at his thoughtfulness but at how easygoing he'd been all day. "Okay," she agreed, wanting to prolong their camaraderie. "It's probably time for the kids to get out anyway."

She climbed from the water, feeling as if she'd put on at least twenty pounds when her feet hit solid ground. Picking up Maddie, she headed for the table. Max followed, carrying Bobby.

They strapped both kids into the high chairs that had

been brought outside. Then soup and sandwiches were served.

"No!" Maddie replied when Kaitland tried to feed her the soup.

"No!" Bobby echoed.

"I thought they'd be hungry," Max said and again offered the soup. Bobby rubbed his eyes and pushed the spoon away.

"They're tired. They've had a full morning. Maybe they'll eat if they can feed themselves," she added. Cutting up one of the sandwiches into small pieces, she set it before the children.

Bobby immediately ate several bites. Maddie had to peel back the bread and examine what was in it, making disgusting faces when the mayonnaise caused the bread to stick to her fingers. She ate the meat inside, though.

With an eye on them, Kaitland sat back and enjoyed the soup.

"I enjoyed this morning, Katie," Max said, tasting his soup.

"The kids are fun," she replied.

"I enjoyed you, too," he added.

Kaitland's spoon paused.

"I've been thinking over what happened the other day," Max said. "I want to apologize for my actions. Rand pointed out to me that I've been pigheaded and I should do my best to let go of the past and get on with my life. I'll be honest. I don't know how well I'll do, but if we could start out working toward one goal, I think we might do it. I'd like to work toward being friends. Maybe if we can just take one day at a time, be civil and promise not to look back, each day it will get easier to forget. I think five years ago, we both ran from the pain instead of confronting it.''

"You ran, Max. Not me."

"But you never bothered to tell me, just pulled away from me at every opportunity."

Tell him, a voice whispered, but she couldn't. She couldn't sound as if she was giving him an excuse for her behavior when it had been so wrong. "You're right. We both made mistakes. All I'm asking is when you find the kids' mother, we part as friends. Nothing more. I'd like that."

Max nodded. "I'd like that, too."

"There's a children's show at the library next week. They're having a clown. It's a lot of fun. I usually volunteer each summer...but you know that."

"I think Maddie and Bobby would like that."

Kaitland smiled. "I'd like that, too." Looking to where Maddie was beginning to nod off, she stood. "I have to get the children up and changed for their nap. You want to help?"

"Sure," Max replied, standing. Something had finally been accomplished. He pushed the fear that she might be involved in the latest blackmail scheme to the back of his mind. He was going to take this one day at a time. Only one day. Everything was fine today, he'd deal with that.

He juggled until he could pick Maddie up.

"Max, you have a phone call from a private investigator. Dugan Lawrence."

Max looked up to where Sarah had appeared. He glanced back to where Kaitland held Bobby and saw the disappointment in her eyes. "Can you do this alone? That's the people who are working on finding the kids' mother."

"Do you think they've found her?"

"I don't know. But Dugan rarely calls in the middle of the day like this. I'd say it's promising."

He started to hand the baby over to Kaitland, but Sarah intercepted her. "I'll take her, Maxwell. You go answer that call."

He smiled. "Thank you, Sarah. I'll be up as soon as I'm off the phone and let you know what they said," he told Kaitland as he turned toward the doors that led to the den.

As he left, he wondered at his feelings. He was excited to be talking with Dugan, but worried, too. His gut was clenched as he wondered if he was about to lose the kids after searching so long for the mother, and he worried about Kaitland, too. They'd just resolved to try to work out their problems. Surely their time wasn't about to end now, was it?

Going into the den, he picked up the phone.

Chapter Fourteen

"**S**he's dead."

"What?" Kaitland stared at Max's strained features.

"That's why Dugan has had so much trouble finding her. The mother is dead. But we do know who she is. Her name was Samantha Jenkins. Dugan traced her back to a shelter for unwed mothers. She evidently was dropped off there by a man late one night, aeons ago. According to the woman at the shelter, Samantha wouldn't say who the father was, just that she wanted to keep the babies, was running from an ex-boyfriend and that a man had picked her up alongside the road and given her a ride."

"You were that man?"

Max nodded. "I was driving home one night and saw her walking along the road. She was huge. I thought she was going to have the babies any minute. She assured me she had a month to go. I bought her a meal, prayed with her, gave her some money."

Max sat down in the outer room of the nursery. "According to Dugan, she had the babies two weeks later, was up on her feet and went to work at a restaurant in town. From what he can find out from her co-workers, Samantha was being harassed by her old boyfriend to go back to whatever she had once done. She didn't want to, so she decided she had to run. Her co-workers said she was afraid he'd use the kids against her—probably why she left them with me.''

"So, who is the father?"

"No one's listed on the birth certificates and she never mentioned his name to anyone."

"So, what are we going to do now?"

"Kaitland, do you suppose we could get your pastor to help us pull some strings and get them temporarily assigned to you, here at my house, just until I can get my lawyers to find someone to adopt them? Or until I get temporarily certified as an emergency foster parent?"

Kaitland's eyes widened. "I might be able to. We'd need to make an appointment with Jake, go in and talk to him. Then we can see what he says."

"Good. Make the appointment for tomorrow. We'll get Darlene to watch the kids.

Kaitland nodded. "I hope you know what you're doing," she replied, but in her heart, she knew he was doing the right thing. He would make sure the children went to a good home. She trusted Max on this.

He stood. "I need to get back to work. Give the kids my love when they wake up."

"I will," she replied, her heart flopping over at his words. Those babies didn't know how much Max loved them yet. Nor, Kaitland was afraid, had Max himself figured it out yet, either.

"So, what is it that you needed to talk to me about?" Jake asked, leaning back in his chair and studying Max and Kaitland.

Max sat with his legs crossed, the picture of elegance in his casual gray suit, while Kaitland wore one of the drop-waist dresses she referred to as her day-care attire. Loose, simple and able to take any stains. Her hair was pulled back in a braid and she squirmed as Jake studied her.

"Kaitland and I have come to you for help," Max said. "I'm not sure if you know that Katie has been an emergency foster parent for years."

Jake smiled. "As a matter of fact, I do. I'm just surprised she told you. Kaitland isn't a very talkative person."

He had been joking, but Max took him seriously, Kaitland could tell by the strange look he shot her. *Oh no,* she thought. *Don't tell him. He doesn't know* you *are the one.* "Katie and I go way back," Max said, not catching the mild panic in her eyes.

She saw the moment Jake made the connection. His smile dropped away and his eyes shot to Katie in shock. Max was still looking at Kaitland so he didn't see her pastor's reaction.

"I've known for a long time she wanted to be a foster parent," he continued. "I even knew her when she filled out the paperwork." A shadow crossed his face before his expression was once again impassive. She knew he was remembering that was just before the ball that had ruined their lives, though she hadn't sent off the paperwork until after their breakup. She'd told Max she wanted to hold on to the documents and pray first.

"You know of the children that were left on my doorstep anonymously," Max said. "We finally found the mother. Unfortunately, she's dead. She was killed in an auto accident in Texas. There's no father listed.''

Jake nodded, then addressed Kaitland, ''What's the problem?''

''We want help talking with the agencies about me keeping the children at Max's house until he can get his lawyers to find someone to adopt them,'' Kaitland said.

Jake looked from one to the other, his hands steepled in front of his lips. Finally, his gaze rested on Max. ''Why?''

Kaitland would have worried over Jake's statement had it been delivered to her in such a blunt tone. But Max, used to big business deals, was unflappable. He uncrossed his legs, folded his hands over his flat stomach and met Jake's stare with one that was deadly serious. ''I feel responsible for these children. The mother left them in my care for a reason. True, I only fed her and gave her a lift to the unwed mothers' home. But in her mind, she felt that was enough to judge me as a responsible person to leave her babies with. I've watched Maddie and Bobby over the last few weeks. They're very attached to each other. If they go into foster care with someone else, it's not guaranteed they'll be kept together...especially if someone adopts them. I'd like to keep them at my house with temporary guardianship until I can get my lawyers working on finding someone to adopt them. I'm rich. In this world, money does talk. I'm willing to use the money to help these children. And though prayer doesn't matter to the world, I do pray and think it's God's will that these children stay here. God tells us we should feed the hungry. I can provide for these children while my lawyers find adoptive parents.''

"And you know it'll take a while to certify Max since he's never been a foster parent, but I'm already certified," Kaitland added.

"Many will assume you wish to adopt because you're the children's natural father, Max. What about your reputation, should this get out?" Jake said. "Or how about Kaitland's reputation?"

Max flinched a tad and Kaitland was sure he was thinking of her reputation with him, or lack thereof. She'd had a sterling reputation once. How those pictures had stayed out of the papers, she didn't know. But the only one who knew she had a soured reputation was Max, and her pastor. And probably Rand. And Elizabeth. The list seemed to be getting longer as the years went by.

"I can't speak for Katie." He gave her an unfathomable look that sent a trickle of worry down her spine. It was as if he was seeing someone else, some other time, and that made him sad. Then his eyes refocused and he was his normal self again. "But you've seen what the magazines print about me. I have a black heart and am a love-'em-and-leave-'em type of guy. Of course, it's not true, but I've learned that any storm can be weathered if you just ignore it. I have to depend on God to fight my battles in that area, though I'm not above calling the TV stations and telling them I'd be most displeased if they ran something particularly obnoxious." He smiled.

Kaitland wondered if he actually realized how powerful he was in the business world. Not everyone could do that. She knew he'd made his displeasure known on several occasions. Of course, the media knew he had the money to sue if they did print lies that hurt his family or business. That's the only time she'd ever seen

Max carry through on a threat. He and Rand would allow no one to touch their family with cruel lies. Many retractions had appeared. But the everyday hounding and petty lies, he tended to ignore.

Knowing if this news hit the papers, who'd have a field day examining his life and those of the children, Kaitland realized Max must be much more wary of the situation than he let on. To keep a scandal at bay, he would need as much secrecy as possible until the arrangements were a fait accompli. And he would see to it, or heads would roll.

"Kaitland?" Jake asked.

"I don't think it'll get out. If it does, no one will be interested in me," she replied. "At least, not that much. I won't be under the pressure Max will be under."

Max and Jake both studied her incredulously. "I can handle it," she replied stubbornly.

"Even if the board hits the ceiling over this?" Jake asked.

"Yes. Even if the board hits the ceiling." She knew two people on the board who would have fits if it came out in the newspapers that she was working for Max. Even though nothing was going on, it would still look bad for the church. She could hear the arguments now: "She's living with a man who has two illegitimate children," they'd say. Kaitland felt sure that Max wasn't the children's father. But, she thought wearily, that would be the popular assumption. How will that look to the parents of the children she is in charge of? What about the moral clause in her contract? How will it effect newcomers to the church if a scandal is cast over this church?

And they were right, to a point. Heaven knew there

had been enough church scandals in the past five years that hit the paper. But, despite how she felt over the possible repercussions, Kaitland knew she had to work out her differences with Max before she could go on with her life. She believed God was in this even if no one else did.

Jake sighed. "Very well. Max, can you give all the information to Shirley and then I'll make some calls."

Max wasn't stupid. He eyed Kaitland before standing. "I'll be out here when you're ready, Katie."

Kaitland nodded.

When the door was closed, Jake's hands fell to his desk. He leaned forward, crossed his arms and stared at her for several moments. "He's the one, isn't he?" Jake finally asked.

Katie had known that was coming. "Yes, he is."

"Why didn't you say something before I sent you to his house?"

Katie shrugged. "I felt it was time to clear the air. It was nothing against you. But you *are* a friend of the Stevens brothers. I thought maybe one of them had mentioned my relationship with Max, until you suggested I go out there."

"Correct me if I'm wrong, dear one. But don't you love him?"

Katie looked around the office, not meeting his eyes. When Jake didn't comment, she finally said, "Okay, yes, you know I do. But I specifically went out there so I could put the past behind me and go on with my life."

"You're setting yourself up in a dangerous situation, you know that, don't you, Kaitland?"

"I don't think you have anything to worry about. Max is no longer interested in me that way."

"I wouldn't be so sure. The air crackled every time he looked at you when you weren't paying attention. He might be hurting, still feel betrayed, but you're a lovely woman, one he planned to marry. I don't want you in a situation where you might end up getting hurt again."

Kaitland sighed. "I know, Jake. I promise. If things get too intense, I'll move out. But we've spent lots of time together since I started caring for the children and nothing has happened."

"Not yet," Jake said. "Just be careful."

There was a pause, then Jake asked softly. "Since you've had time with him, have you told Max everything yet?"

She flushed. "No. I'm not sure he'd forgive me even if I did tell him."

He studied Kaitland before finally saying, "Then maybe you just need to forgive him for his mistakes and leave it at that. We can't make anyone forgive us. And yes, you should have told him when it happened, but no one's perfect. If Max can't understand that and is still angry with you, then he's not the man for you. God will have someone else for you."

Jake came around the desk and took her hands. "I'm here, Kaitland, if you need me. Day or night, just give me a call."

Kaitland smiled. "Thank you."

"Let me make some calls."

She went to the door. Outside, Max was waiting for her. They walked out into the main sanctuary while they waited for Jake to make his calls. "What did Jake want?"

Kaitland sighed, dropped her head back and stared up at the vaulted ceiling. She'd love to lean just a little to her right and rest her head on Max's shoulder, but knew he wouldn't accept her need for security right now. Instead, she answered him honestly, blunting any emotions from her voice. "He didn't know you were the one I was engaged to until you mentioned it to him. He wanted to make sure I had made the right decision in staying out there with you."

"Wise man."

Kaitland turned to look at him in surprise.

"We were engaged once, Katie. Of course your pastor would be worried about the situation. And you can't deny that the attraction between us is still there. Otherwise, I wouldn't be tempted to kiss you at the most inopportune moments."

Seeing the look in his eyes, she realized this was one of those moments. He reached up and touched a loose strand of her hair. "We're both adults," she argued. "And besides, what good is attraction if there's no trust."

Max sighed, a resigned look coming to his eyes. "You're right. Without trust there's no reason to carry anything further, is there?"

Ask me why. Just ask me why, she wanted to say. Instead, he only stared at her. "No," she whispered, her gut churning as she fought and tried to tell him, then finally lost the battle. "No, no reason at all."

They sat in silence in the darkened church, the only noise from the day-care children in the background and the occasional sound of beeping from the computer in Shirley's office.

"By the way," Max said casually, looking at the nails on his right hand instead of at her, which immediately warned Kaitland she wasn't going to like what he had to say.

"Yes?" she asked when he paused.

"There is a car being delivered to the house tomorrow."

She knew immediately where this was going. She saw red. "I told you, Maxwell Edward Stevens, that I wouldn't—"

"Now, che'rie," he said, smiling congenially and holding up his hands. "I worked on your car, remember? What type of person would I be if I let you drive around in that—especially with the children in it."

"But—"

"Just think," he interrupted. "Your car is, unfortunately, a breakdown waiting to happen. What would happen if you were on the road with the kids, followed by a reporter...or at night and followed by something worse. Please accept the gift. It's not a too expensive car that would embarrass you as a gift."

Kaitland softened at those words. Even when they still had those problems between them, he was thinking of her, and what people might say if he were to give her a very expensive car. "Oh, Max," she said, dropping her head.

"Please, che'rie. Please accept the car."

She struggled. Pride wanted her to say no. But he had a good argument. "You chose your words carefully, using the kids against me, didn't you?"

He smiled a boyishly handsome smile. "It worked, didn't it?"

Reluctantly she smiled. "Yes, it worked." But it worked even better on her heart. She realized how much she truly loved this man. Not as in past tense, but now, and that she would somehow, sometime, find the courage to tell him about what happened because maybe, just maybe, he might actually be ready to understand what had happened five years ago. She hadn't thought so until now. But whether he'd meant it to or not, his concern had shown her a glimpse into his heart. The man she thought she'd known was still there, just buried under a lot of excess baggage that he had to get rid of. Exactly what it all entailed, she didn't know. But maybe they could work this all out.

"Please, Father," she whispered.

Twenty minutes passed before Jake came walking out of his office.

He propped a foot on the pew in front of him and rested his arms across his knee. "Well, it's done. Believe it or not, all I had to do was mention your name, Max, and people bent over backward. You'll have to tell Rand I might be using his name in the future when I'm dealing with some hardheaded businessman." He grinned and Max chuckled.

"I'll do that."

"The papers will be drawn up. Your lawyers should contact the social worker on the case and then you'll have documents to sign and, to make a long story short, it looks like you'll get to keep the kids without losing them any time soon. They'll process the paperwork to certify you as a foster parent just in case Kaitland wants to leave."

Kaitland flushed, knowing it was an out Jake had suggested. "Meanwhile, you need to take the children to the doctor. According to the people I spoke with, there are probably some shots and stuff the kids need, plus social services will need a medical record on file of the kids' health."

Max stood. He stuck out his hand. "Thanks, Jake. Rand was certain you'd help us, but I had my doubts, especially with our past." He glanced to Kaitland.

"Yeah, well, about that. I'll reserve judgment and trust that since both of you are Christians, you'll put God first in your relationship—or lack of one," he added when Kaitland started to object. "Just as long as you put God first."

"We'll do that," Max said. Grabbing Kaitland by the hand, he pulled her up to stand beside him. Jake, of course, didn't miss that. Kaitland's heart didn't, either, though she tried to act nonchalant. She was disappointed when he released her and placed a hand to her back. "We'll go make a doctor's appointment for the kids right now and have them examined by my store's physician. A family doctor should be all right, I suppose. I mean, they don't have to go to a pediatrician today, do they?"

Jake chuckled. "Any doctor will be fine. Family doctors handle kids, too."

"Good. Well, you take care and hopefully we'll bring the children to this church to visit sometime soon. We've been looking around for a new church, Rand and I. He suggested Elizabeth's church."

"We'd be glad to have you," Jake said.

"Thanks again, Jake."

Kaitland breathed a sigh of relief as they exited the sanctuary.

"Now what?" she asked as he held the passenger-side door of the Mercedes open for her.

"Now, my dear Kaitland," he said, resting his hand on the door and dropping to where he could meet her eyes, "We get to play doctor."

Chapter Fifteen

"No, no, bad!" Maddie slapped the stethoscope away from her chest, frowning severely at the elderly doctor who was trying to do the examination.

Max had gotten quite an education about children and doctors while he was here. "Come on, che'rie," Max cooed. "Be nice."

Her lower lip jutted out. Bobby, who was confined to Kaitland's lap while he waited for his turn on the examining table, jutted out his lip, too. "Baaaaad!" he bellowed then clapped.

Dr. Weston laughed, and put his listening device back into his pocket. "They both seem to be in fine health and very well developed for their age. This little one has quite a stubborn streak, doesn't she?"

Dr. Weston lowered Maddie to the ground to watch her walk as he began filling out the paperwork. Max wasn't surprised when she toddled over to the plant on the floor and tried to eat it. "No, no, Maddie, dear," the doctor began.

"Mine!"

Max lifted Maddie into his arms, dug the plant out of her mouth, ignoring the teeth that clamped down on his finger. "Don't worry. She usually doesn't swallow it, unless you leave it in there very long. She just likes plants."

Weston chuckled again. "Well, she can like them, but teach her not to eat them. Some are poisonous."

"Believe me, I know. I've had my gardener go through the house and get rid of any that are. I'm having my gardens redone where the children might come in contact with any of them, too."

"I'm glad to hear that. Each year poisoning is a danger for young children." He turned back to the children and smiled kindly. "She's walking fine. So is Bobby. The only thing left are the shots."

Max tensed. He felt harried after an hour at the doctor's office. They'd pulled two bugs from Bobby's mouth, and taken away a bottle that Maddie had snatched from a baby. Then, of course, he had made the mistake of taking a turn holding Bobby while Maddie was examined and Bobby had christened him again. He was getting good at holding the child at arm's length. Max was afraid Bobby thought it was some game and peed on him just to be thrust out in midair. He always chortled afterward.

Max decided he was going to invent a diaper that didn't leak, except he figured Bobby would find some way around it.

And now he had to wait for the children to get shots. He knew they would throw a fit—especially Maddie. "Are the shots necessary?" he asked.

"I'm afraid so. These are their first shots, their MMR. It's more important to get the shots than risk the diseases."

"I understand," Max said, resigned. The doctor nodded and left.

"Don't worry," Kaitland reassured Max as they waited in the small room. "They'll do fine."

Just then a nurse walked in with two injections in her hand. The doctor stuck his head in behind her. "I'll fax this paperwork to the office that needs it and you can go when Colleen is done."

Max thanked the doctor, who immediately went back out the door. The coward. Pronounce his sentence then leave the kids for the parents and nurse to handle. "How do you want them? On the table?"

The nurse smiled. "No. You hold the little girl, I'll inject her in the thigh."

Max nodded. He gathered Maddie close. He loved the way Maddie smelled like powder and was so soft. He rubbed his nose against her silky hair, before wrapping his arms around her.

He wasn't sure if he could do this. Until now, the children had been something special, exciting, sweet. But this was different. He didn't want to cause them pain. He knew, logically, that it was necessary, but the thought of them going through any more than they had already...

"Max, do you want me to hold her?" Kaitland stared, concerned, noting the way he was stroking Maddie's head and how she was gurgling.

"No. I just hate that she'll feel more pain." He looked at the nurse and nodded. "There's going to be a little stick, che'rie, then Max will make it all better," he whispered.

He saw the needle descend.

Suddenly Maddie's eyes widened and her face crumpled. A loud wail broke from her throat. She sounded as if her world was ending. "It's okay, che'rie," he whispered, patting her back. "Max loves you and will take care of you."

His heart rose to his throat when he realized what he'd said, *Max loves you.* It was true. In the few weeks they'd been with him, the kids had become more than just a responsibility but two people he loved and cared deeply about. "Max loves you, che'rie," he whispered again, patting her back.

Her cries turned to whimpers and suddenly, against his cheek, he felt a tiny hand patting him. "Me love," she blubbered through tears. "Me love."

"I love you, too," he whispered again and again and she continued to pat his cheek and he her back.

Another wail filled the room and he looked over to see Bobby's face crumpled into a scowl as he wailed out his displeasure. It was funny how he could tell the differences. Where Maddie had been truly distressed, Bobby was just plain mad.

"Come here, Bobby," Max said, surprising Kaitland. Of course Kaitland was surprised. He avoided holding Bobby because of Bobby's leaky bladder every time he picked him up. He held open his arm and Bobby willingly flung himself into his embrace. Maddie patted Bobby, "Bobu, Bobu," she repeated over and over and Max hugged him close until the little boy's wails ceased. In seconds Bobby was gurgling and talking his baby gibberish to his sister.

He heard Kaitland thanking the nurse and then she gathered up the diaper bags. He stood there holding the kids, feeling like an idiot, but soaking in their presence.

After weeks, it was disconcerting to think he wanted these children to be his own, that he was actually disappointed that they weren't. His heart felt protective over the idea of them getting shots, over what they wore, what they ate. Looking back, he realized he'd slowly been falling in love all along.

Seeing Kaitland walk up, he thought that if they'd gotten married years ago as they'd planned, his kids would be around four years old by now. Kaitland had wanted kids immediately. Was that why she liked being a foster mother? Why hadn't she had kids?

Those new questions rose in his mind, questions he'd never asked himself before, as well as old ones of why had she been sleeping with someone else when she was engaged to him? She was a Christian. He just couldn't mesh the two images. She believed in chastity and they both had agreed to wait, yet the pictures showed, to the contrary, that she hadn't waited.

Maddie patted his cheek again, drawing him back to the kids. He couldn't desert them. How did he know they would be adopted by someone who loved them? How could he trust someone to take care of them right? How could he live without them?

"You're gonna have a hard time letting them go," Kaitland said, as if reading his mind.

"No, I'm not," he replied.

Going to the door, he arranged payment and left.

"Of course you are, Max. I can tell just by looking at you how attached you're becoming to these kids."

They strapped the kids into the car seats then climbed into the front seat.

"You're right, but I'm not letting them go. I'm going to adopt them."

Kaitland stared, aghast. "But how? Why? I mean, I know you care for them, Max. But you're not married."

There was a heartbeat of silence, then Max replied, "You don't have to tell me that."

She didn't recoil even though his words hurt. "I meant they should have a father *and* a mother."

"They have no one right now."

"But maybe, with time, someone can be found..."

"*With time* being the operative words. I've been thinking. They're getting used to me, and how can you guarantee that we can find someone who will take them both? That's going to be hard. Plus, once we do find adoptive parents, can you guarantee they'll love the twins and make sure they have what they need?"

He backed out of the parking lot and pointed the car toward home.

Kaitland knew he wasn't talking material possessions. Max wasn't that shallow. Still, it rankled that he could adopt these children if he wanted, and probably be accepted as a parent.

With shock, she realized the reason the idea bothered her was that she wasn't in the picture, too. Ashamed, she looked off into the distance. He had made his choice a long time ago. The past was over.

"You care for them now, Max. But isn't it possible that when you marry, your wife wouldn't?"

"I wouldn't marry someone who couldn't love my children."

She knew that. She wasn't thinking clearly. "What if you get tired of them? I mean, it'll be just you. Will you grow bored with all of the childhood diseases and sibling rivalry that goes on. And two get into more mischief than one."

"I think I, of all people, would know that. Remember the trouble Rand was always getting me into. And boy, was it something else. Yes, I think I'm qualified to understand the workings of twins.''

He was right there.

"But how is your brother going to take it?"

Max smiled. "He'll be enthused, I'm sure."

"You're going to what?" Rand's voice rose and Kaitland watched as, with effort, Rand forced himself to calm down. "I knew you'd been going through something the last week or so, but I didn't think it was that." He glanced toward Kaitland then back, indicating just what he'd thought it was.

"It's what I think is best all around. Samantha Jenkins left her children with me. They have no one now. I want children." He shrugged. "I'll love them."

Kaitland could tell Rand struggled before finally nodding. "I'll have the lawyers get on it immediately."

Kaitland was surprised Rand took this so easily. But then she remembered the special link the brothers shared. Rand evidently knew more about what Max was feeling than she did.

However, Elizabeth wasn't so quiet. "I think you're avoiding the real issue here, Max," she said, glaring at him as if she was an older sister about to chastise a child.

Max scowled at her. "And that is?"

"Your heart. You want a family, and are opting for the easy way instead of letting God heal you first."

Max's scowl turned darker. He shot a look at Kaitland then back to Elizabeth. "That, my dear, is none of your business."

Elizabeth opened her mouth to argue. Kaitland saw Rand unobtrusively reach over and lay a hand on Elizabeth's thigh. She closed her mouth a moment, then said, "I'm family. But you're right. There are other ways to handle this." She grinned cheekily. "I'll just pray for you and God will work it all out."

Max groaned. "One day, Elizabeth... Rand, you must talk to your wife about her mouth."

Rand grinned, turning his eyes down on Elizabeth. "Oh, I will, brother, as soon as I get her upstairs."

Elizabeth blushed.

Max cleared his throat.

Kaitland looked away from the loving stare Rand gave Elizabeth.

"Excuse me, please," Kaitland said. "I need to go check on the kids and then run by my house. I'll see you later."

She turned and left, unable to bear the banter anymore.

"She still loves you."

Max glanced to Elizabeth, who, he saw, had been watching him watch Kaitland leave.

"I care for her, too," he told his sister-in-law. "And before you start nagging again, Kaitland and I are trying to work past the hurt so we can be friends again."

"Just friends?" Rand asked, studying Max with concern.

"If she would only talk to me, maybe, just maybe I could begin to understand her betrayal. I could never trust her again, but I could at least let go of the pain."

"Have you asked her what happened, Max?"

"No, Elizabeth. I don't think I can."

"Why?"

"Because..." Because why? Because Max was afraid of her answers. It might destroy the wall around his heart? He'd have to face that he might have been wrong in his judgment? Why? Exasperated, refusing to face the questions, he said, "Nothing. I need to go see to some things Jennifer was going to fax over to me."

He got up and headed to the library, thinking about not only what his sister-in-law had said just now, but earlier, too. He was afraid Kaitland would say something like she didn't love him, or had decided she really didn't want to marry him. He was almost certain she was here to search out forgiveness for something she'd done. Guilt was a powerful motivator. If that were true, then they might be able to get over everything and be friends, but it would soon be obvious that love wasn't motivating her at all, only the guilt. How did you bare your heart to someone like that? She very well might say she loved him and they'd be in the same mess again. He found he really didn't want to face whatever she might have to say. And what if she said something else? Was he ready to deal with part of what had really driven him to let her go in the first place? Could he bare that part of him to anyone?

As for the kids... Yes, he wanted kids of his own. Elizabeth was right about that. And he yearned to have them, something a bachelor wasn't suppose to admit to. But that wasn't the only reason he wanted to adopt Maddie and Bobby. There Elizabeth was wrong. He loved them. He would one day have children if he married.

Bobby and Maddie would be as much his as any other children. He didn't believe in separating out the kids as some did, calling them stepkids, or adopted kids. They would be *his* kids. As far as he was concerned, he would accept them as if they were flesh of his flesh. And as much as he could he would protect those kids from the media and any other negative effects. Unlike his father, who had been unable to protect

Rand and himself from the many harsh realities of what the media could do to destroy a family. Or the realities of a mother who got so caught up in the negative effect of a media exposure that all she could think about was getting out.

He forced his mind away from that past sorrow. Instead, he thought about the kids.

Elizabeth would see in time that he could provide for the children. Max thought Rand might actually have glimpsed that determination in Max's spirit or he would have objected more. As for Kaitland…the future was a blank where she was concerned. She would see his determination…if she was here long enough.

Kaitland.

What was he going to do about the dark murky situation with her?

Chapter Sixteen

"Hello there, little one!" Max scooped Bobby up off the floor and held him above his head. "What's say we go celebrate?"

Kaitland grinned with indulgence. The last few days she'd seen a change in Max. He was no longer the moody, careful man around her, he was more the carefree person she'd once known. They had come to an uneasy truce and were doing their best to forget the past and become friends again.

The only problem was, she couldn't sleep at night for the memories that haunted her. Over and over the near rape played in her mind. She and Max could play at being friends, but there was always going to be a small barrier between them because of the one small piece of the puzzle she held. Yet, if she revealed it to him, she wouldn't be able to stand the disgust on his face. Or worse, she might have to face that he wouldn't believe her. So, she held the missing link in her heart and prayed God would provide the opportune moment for her to reveal it.

In the meantime, they both did their best to talk and act as if nothing were wrong. If they practiced long enough, she hoped that Max would open up and she would find a way to explain the past to him.

Now, she simply pushed the unpleasantness behind her and smiled. "What has you in such a good mood?"

Max grinned at her as he put Bobby down and lifted Maddie who was demanding his attention. "My lawyers called. They've started adoption proceedings. I feel like celebrating and thought I'd take the kids to a fast-food restaurant."

"When was the last time you went to a place like that?" Kaitland questioned, amused.

"There's a first time for everything, isn't there? I remember seeing playgrounds there. We could take the kids, feed them, let them play, then bring them back and put them down for a nap."

She laughed at Max's hopeful expression. "And then?"

"And then some peace and quiet. You and I could play Scrabble on the patio or just sit and enjoy the spring day. Sound good to you?"

Kaitland smiled. It sounded heavenly. Max was putting forth the effort and she would go along with him. "I'd love to. Just let me fill the diaper bags."

"I'll drive. I don't want to look too obvious with a chauffeur." He put Maddie down. She objected loudly and hung on to his leg.

"If you don't want to look obvious, I'd suggest you change out of your casual suit."

He grinned. "I've bought new clothes. Meet me in the library and you'll see. After all, I can't afford to buy new shirts and slacks every time this one wets on me," he said, glancing down at Bobby who had toddled over to the toy box. Maddie let go of Max's leg and followed Bobby.

Kaitland shook her head. "Cotton?"

"Right from the JCPenney catalog."

"I'll believe it when I see it, Max."

She changed and dressed the children then packed the diaper bags.

Taking the children by the hands, she escorted them down the stairs to Max's library. Maddie, who had taken a fancy to the plant in this particular room, toddled right over to where it should have been. But it wasn't there. In consternation, the little girl began to explore the room—looking for the plant, no doubt. Bobby went to the coffee table and began to remove the magazines one by one.

Kaitland sighed, gathered up the magazines to move them, but was interrupted. "Well, how do I look?"

Kaitland turned, and gaped. *Gorgeous,* she thought. Tan cotton pants and a berry shirt tucked into them with a slim dark belt circling his middle. It was a shame that any man could be so gorgeous.

"Well, well, well..."

Kaitland heard Rand's voice and looked beyond Max to find Rand gaping in astonishment, too. Rand came in and made a show of circling Max. "Little brother has decided to finally discard the swinging-bachelor image, I see. Where did you get these clothes?"

Max glared at his brother. "Penney's. And they're fine. They're washable. I made sure of that."

"Oh, I'm not saying that at all, little bro. What I am saying is that it's about time. I just never thought to see my brother give up his wardrobe of Armani suits for cotton knit and permanent press."

"Well, now you have, so stop harassing me and go find your wife. I'm sure she'd appreciate your humor. She did enough while you were ill to get you laughing again."

The brothers stared at each other a moment and Kaitland could tell they were doing that twin thing again that she'd often witnessed—communicating without saying a word. Then Rand smiled and said, "You look good," and walked out.

"Maddie and Bobby do that, too."

"Do what?" Max asked, coming over and scooping up Maddie, blowing strawberries on her stomach before settling her on his hip.

"That silent-communication thing."

Max glanced at Kaitland in surprise, then he smiled and there was a mystery to his eyes as he said, "It's just always been that way between us. I tend to forget that's not common with other people. Rand just...well, he was letting me know he approved of the changes in me."

"It's important what he thinks, isn't it?" Kaitland asked.

"Yeah. Very. I don't know what I'd do if I ever lost Rand. That's one reason I want to adopt Maddie and Bobby. They shouldn't be separated."

"Does it bother you or Elizabeth—your relationship with Rand?"

"Nah. Elizabeth understands. She's not the jealous type. As a matter of fact, she really likes being part of a close, loving family. I'm afraid if I marry, Elizabeth will put the woman through the third degree before she'll allow it."

He strode out the front door and to the car Phil had

brought around. He now had car seats that were transferred to whichever car the twins were going to be in.

Both children were placed in the back seat and strapped in. Then Max slid behind the wheel and they were off. In minutes they were at a fast-food restaurant. "So, what do you want to eat?" he asked, going inside.

Kaitland watched him study the menu. "This is all fried stuff," he muttered.

Kaitland laughed. "It's fast-food. What do you expect?"

"And there's really no choice. Hamburgers or hamburgers," he added.

"They have chicken sandwiches, too. Stop being so critical."

"The food isn't good for kids."

Kaitland rolled her eyes. "One meal isn't going to kill them."

She stepped to the cash register. "Let me order." Without waiting for a reply, she ordered for all four of them. Max paid and then smiled his thanks when a young lady took the tray to the table for them.

He strapped Bobby, who was closest to him, into the high chair and then dug out the hamburgers from their wrappings. In consternation, he stared at Bobby then at the burger. "He can't eat this."

"Like this, Max," Kaitland replied. She tore the hamburger into tiny finger pieces and laid two or three in front of Maddie. The burger was joined by two fries.

Max followed her instructions. "They're making a mess," he added when a piece of bread went over the tray and onto the floor.

"Don't worry. Grab a bite of your hamburger before one of them starts complaining and wanting down. We don't have help here to take them while we finish our meal."

Max bit into his hamburger. His forehead wrinkled. "This is very poor-quality food, but good."

Kaitland rolled her eyes again. "Yes, it's good. And it's not *poor*-quality, Max. It's just different from what you've always eaten."

"I've eaten out," he complained.

"How many times have you eaten in a fast-food restaurant."

Max opened his mouth, then paused. "Once or twice, I'm sure, as a teenager. Rand used to love this stuff and would drag me with him. But I can't remember what restaurant it was."

Max took another bite.

"Dink!"

Bobby pounded his tray then pointed. "Dink! Dink! Dink!"

"Stop that," Kaitland admonished. "Yes, you may have a drink."

Bobby chortled then latched on to the straw Kaitland stuck between his lips.

"Dink! Dink!" Maddie called.

Kaitland turned to Maddie and gave her a drink, too. Max set down his food, helped Bobby, then went back to eating.

It was soon apparent this was how the entire meal was going to go. "I see now why parents sometimes look so frazzled when they come into Stevens Inc. They're full and we haven't even finished half of our meal. But the stress of trying to answer to these two demanding fiends has robbed me of my appetite."

"Save your food in the bag. We'll take it with us

outside. Once they start sliding, you might find you're still hungry.''

They wrapped their food, cleaned up the messy kids, then went out to the playground.

Kaitland took off their shoes and helped both children into the plastic-ball tent. Max smiled as the children squealed and threw balls into the air. ''Why didn't they have stuff like this when we were kids?'' he asked, grinning over their exuberance.

''They had skateboards.''

Max groaned. ''I remember. I have an ankle that aches to remind me of how much we enjoyed skateboards as kids.''

''Why do I hear a story in this?''

''Did I ever break a bone that Rand wasn't somehow behind it?''

''According to you. But one day I'd like to hear Rand's side to all of these stories you tell me.''

''He thought it would be fun to tie ropes to Dad's car bumper, and when he left for work we could catch a ride. At the end of the driveway, we'd let go and see who went the farthest. However, we hadn't thought about the way the driveway curved. Or the trees that lined it.''

''What happened?''

''I was scraped and bruised from the low-hanging branch of one of those historic oaks outside my house, and my ankle was broken in three places. But Rand took the blame and he stayed with me the entire time I was in a cast. It ruined both of our summers.''

Max watched Kaitland laugh. She was beautiful when she relaxed and enjoyed the situation. He couldn't remember her being this beautiful or carefree so many years ago. She'd loved him, but had been so awed by his money. He worried again that it had been his fault she had turned away from him. And wondered as he had at least a thousand times, if it had been for the best. Had he married her back then, no matter how much he had loved her, he had to wonder if she would be this self-assured now, this carefree. Or would she have come to resent living in a glass house?

She was dressed in a loose top and floral full skirt. Her hair was again in a French braid, from which tendrils escaped, softening her features. He wanted to reach out and touch her cheek.

Lifting his hands, he almost did exactly that...until Maddie squealed, "Slide!"

"Are they old enough?" Max immediately asked, eyeing the slide with a little trepidation. "I don't want them to fall."

"We'll stand at the end and catch them. Don't worry."

Kaitland reached in and helped Maddie and Bobby out of the balls. Holding their hands, she walked them over to the slide.

With great patience she guided them up the slide. "Go!" she called out, smiling when Maddie edged her rump to the edge of the slide.

She walked to the end, waiting. Max came up beside her. She stepped forward, to catch the kids and misstepped. Automatically reacting, Max caught her in his arms. "You okay?" he asked, holding her gently in his embrace.

Her pupils dilated just slightly and her breathing was shallow. Max recognized the signals she was sending out. He wanted to kiss her, too. But not here, not in a public place where she might regret it.

"I'm fine," she finally said.

Hearing a squeal, they both turned toward the slide where Maddie came sliding down, feet in the air. Max dropped his arms and scooped up Maddie, just in time, too, for Bobby was right behind her.

Kaitland started to step forward and winced. Immediately, without thinking, Max slipped his arm around Kaitland again. "You okay, Katie?"

"When I misstepped earlier I must have sprained my ankle a bit. I'll be fine."

He watched the yearning in her eyes, saw her bring it under control and then break away. He allowed it. He knew she still cared, that it wasn't just guilt leading her down this road. And it gave him hope.

He would wait for the right time and then find out what Kaitland hid in her heart, what had driven her to betray him as she had, and he would pray that God could heal the breach between them and they could have more.

She scooped up Bobby, kissed him on the cheek and walked them both back to the slide again.

Yes, he was going to pray more for Kaitland. Because Kaitland had too much love in her not to open up and share it with those kids—and him. Despite the resolve, there was a small niggling doubt that reminded him that his mom and dad had once had that, too. He pushed the thought aside. That no longer mattered. Kaitland had gone through the fire just as he had when he'd received those pictures. They could survive anything the media threw at them. She wouldn't eventually get tired of him and the kids and want to leave.

But as much as he believed that, he watched Kaitland as she laughed when the kids both came barreling down the slide again. Would she be able to love him and be willing to stay with him no matter what?

Chapter Seventeen

"So, sister, have you quit working for Max already?"

Kaitland whirled from her car to find her brother sitting on the porch swing.

"Where's your car?"

"In the garage. I didn't want tree sap on it."

She pulled out her keys and opened the door to her house. "So, what brings you here?" she asked, going into the dark interior of the house, already knowing what brought him here, realizing she was going to have to face him after she had been purposely ducking his calls since going to work for Max.

"Why haven't you returned any of my calls? I needed to talk to you last week. It was urgent."

Kaitland went to the rolltop desk in her living room, her low heels clicking across the wooden floor before she crossed onto the rug. She sorted through the bills, placing each in its place, thinking she was finally seeing a light at the end of the tunnel. Just one more week and she'd have enough to pay off the last of the creditors and then she could work on building up savings. She knew she only had two weeks left with Max. She thanked God things had worked out the way they had.

"Kaitland! You're not listening."

She sighed. "Yes, Robert, I am. You said it was urgent. Your urgency wouldn't have anything to do with that dinner party I read about last Saturday?"

Robert flushed and looked petulant when he said, "I'm in between girlfriends. I really needed an escort."

"What happened this time?" Kaitland felt sorry for Robert. He didn't seem to be able to hold down a relationship and she blamed herself in a way. If only she could have helped him understand that she and Grandma had loved him.

"She just didn't work out. I haven't found anyone I like as much as my last girlfriend who left me a year and a half ago. They're all so self-centered. I've had to hire other women to help me and that gets expensive."

Kaitland's eyes widened in dismay. "You've hired professional escorts to go with you to these dinners?"

"What did you expect? I can't do this alone."

"Do what alone?"

Robert stopped whining and his face closed up. "Dating," he said. "What do you think? It wouldn't hurt you to answer my calls once in a while and just go with me. You're a good distraction. They all love you."

Memories of that night long ago returned. "Well, I don't like the shallowness of most of the people who attend those functions. We've been through this before. I don't drink. I don't like flirting. I just don't fit in with the rich crowd."

"You seem to be doing okay with your boyfriend,"

he muttered, his countenance turning red as his temper rose.

"What do you mean? I don't have any boyfriend right now."

Robert shot her a dirty look. "Just a minute." He stormed through the house to the side door that led to the garage. Kaitland followed to the kitchen where he was already coming back in. "I'm tired of you lying to me and treating me like pond scum, Kaitland. I'm your own brother and you won't do me one little favor. But I just wonder what type of favors you've been doing him."

He slammed three different papers down on the counter.

"Oh dear heavens," Kaitland whispered, her face draining of color. The top paper was a national rag magazine that showed her in Max's embrace. And they certainly did look cozy. Her eyes were half-closed, her lips parted, and Max was leaning close as if he had just kissed her or was about to. It looked very, very intimate. Wedding Bells Ringing, the headline read. The day at the fast-food restaurant, she realized bleakly.

Quickly, she moved the magazine aside to find another one. On it, was another picture of her and Max. He was holding Maddie in his arms and had an arm around her. Stevens' Secret Family, it was captioned.

The third picture showed Max holding Bobby above his head, her in the background with Maddie. Bachelor Father, the headline read.

As she scanned each article, she found three different stories. She was his mistress and these were his children; she was his wife and was kept hidden because she wasn't rich enough to be accepted by Max's crowd;

she was the live-in nanny and she was helping with the kids but Max and her had a thing going and were planning marriage.

"Well?" Robert demanded.

She looked up, her head whirling at the thought of what this was going to do to her reputation and Max's, as well. "I've got to call Max."

"You don't deny this?" Robert pointed toward the papers.

"Of course I do, not that it's any business of yours."

"I'm your brother," Robert argued. "Of course I have a right to know. You won't help me out, but you're willing to ruin my position as a lobbyist by having your name splashed all over the front page of these national magazines."

"Trash-zines," she corrected, going toward the phone. "And don't try your guilt on me. You'll revel in this at your work. The more notoriety, good or bad, the better known you are and the more likely people will know your name."

Robert advanced, furious. "Don't push me, Kaitland. You and that grandmother of yours got everything. Everything. I was left with practically nothing. I'm trying to make a living at a very difficult job. And you, who professes to be so loving and kind, won't even help me when I ask it."

"You're rich, Robert."

Robert's eyes narrowed. "Not in my circles I'm not. According to those I hang around with, I'm an upstart with barely enough money to qualify for their clubs. Certain things are expected of me. And to see me escorting my sister around would certainly help my reputation, even if she is a tease." He swung his arms at the photos. "You're right about that. But that doesn't mean I have to accept your actions when you've all but ignored me."

Kaitland's temper sparked. "I don't have time for this, Robert. I'm due back at work by two so Darlene can have the rest of the week off. If you don't mind, I have some phone calls to make."

"You're throwing me out?" he asked incredulously.

"Unless you have something nice to say, I'm asking you to leave. You know I've never thrown you out."

He turned and stormed out the door. She heard his car start and then the engine roar as he shot out of the driveway.

She was immediately contrite. He was her only brother, whether he was blood or not. She shouldn't have talked to him that way. He always sought her out to blow off steam.

She sighed. Had she not been so upset over the pictures, she wouldn't have lost her temper. Now she was going to have to apologize. She also understood why the scriptures said not to be unequally yoked, believers with unbelievers. She couldn't imagine being married to someone who was like her brother.

At least Robert looked better, as if he was off the alcohol now. And she hadn't smelled any on his breath. Yet he was on a course of self-destruction and she didn't know how she could turn him around. Need. He always needed more money, more power, more favor with the senators... It was going to ruin him if he didn't get control of himself.

The phone rang, sounding loud in the quiet house. "Hello?"

"Katie. I've been trying to catch you all morning."

"Max." Tired and now worried how she would handle this new problem, she sighed.

"You've seen," he said curtly.

Kaitland leaned back against the couch. "Yes, I've seen. So, what do we do about it?"

"Are you okay?" His fury subsided and concern echoed across the phone lines, warming Kaitland's heart. "I didn't mean for this to happen. You know how those reporters hound my family."

"I'll be fine. I guess I'm still in shock. And Robert was here when I arrived…"

"What did Robert want?"

"Don't sound so sour, Max. He's my brother."

"Stepbrother who enjoys using you. He hurts you every time he's around, Katie. I can't help worrying whenever you bring up his name."

"He was upset over the headlines. That's all. But at least he told me before I found out from some reporter who might have managed to track me down or something."

"You need to come back over here. We have security. You'll be better protected. I'll get to the bottom of this, and make sure there are retractions printed."

"Max, please. It'll only flame the fires."

"I won't let them get away with this. I can't help it, Katie, but I draw the line at my personal life being splashed across the papers…especially when it might jeopardize the adoption proceedings."

Kaitland shivered at the renewed coldness in his voice. She knew from experience Max was not a person to cross when he used that tone.

"Come back and let me handle this," he said, his voice almost abrupt. "They won't bother you here."

"I'm fine, Max. I have bills I must pay. Then I have a few more things I need to do. I'll be back over after that. Don't worry about me."

There was a pause on the other end. "But I do. And soon, Katie, very soon, I think you're gonna figure that out and either open up to me or run away again."

"I didn't run away the first time, Max," Kaitland replied, her heart rate accelerating.

Her breathing turned shallow and her stomach clenched. She could tell by the silence on the other end that Max regretted confronting her so directly. "I want to tell you, Max. I want to tell you everything. But you'll hate me when I do and I just can't face that."

Finally, he sighed. "When you feel the time is right, then. I think I might just want more than friendship. My feelings are becoming more involved and I need to know if we have anything else before it's too late and I open my heart completely to you again."

Tears filled Kaitland's eyes and streamed down her face. "I don't know, Max. I really don't know." She heard a beep and latched on to that as an excuse to get off the phone. "My other line is beeping. I'll see you later this afternoon."

"As you wish."

She clicked to the other line. "Kaitland? This is Jake. I think we need to talk."

Kaitland sighed. She'd known this was coming, had in fact been going to call her pastor before the phone had rung. "When would be a good time to stop by?"

"I'm here all day."

"I'll be right by." She hung up the phone.

What had started out as a nice day was rapidly deteriorating. She wondered if it could get any worse.

"What in the world is going on?"

Bewildered, Kaitland stared at Rand, who was laughing his head off, to Elizabeth who was punching him in the arm, crying, "Stop laughing and help him," just before she herself giggled again, only to repeat the process.

Several of the staff stood behind them, all gawking into the children's nursery.

Kaitland set down her purse and papers and edged her way around the gaping servants. "Max, what are you doing on the floor? Where are the children?"

Max lay on his back near the low-set twin bed that was kept in the room in case she wanted to lie down with the children. His left arm was extended, and on his face he wore a look of extreme frustration. "The…children…are right—" *huff* "— here."

"What's in your hair?" she asked when she noticed his hair was sticking up on end.

"Vaseline."

A high-pitched giggle escaped from under the bed and Kaitland realized the children were ducking Max's grasp. "What happened?"

"What does it look like?" he questioned, making another foray with his hand under the bed, which brought another round of giggles from the two culprits.

"It looks like they're playing hide-and-seek."

Max paused to stare incredulously at her.

She sighed. "Grab a shirt and reel one in, the other will follow."

"I would, if they were wearing any clothes," he said tightly.

"He's been at this at least five minutes now," Rand said, doing his best to remove the grin from his face and failing miserably.

"You see," Max continued, moving his hand back and forth as he ignored his brother's words, "evidently, Bobby finally learned to undress himself. As you know,

Maddie is already proficient. And I was only gone from the room a minute…''

"And they slipped under the bed." Rand chuckled again.

"Can't you snag an ankle?" she asked, a little alarmed at the shade of Max's face.

"Oh, he has, several times. That's what's the matter with his hair. What Max isn't telling you," Rand said, "is that the little angels found the Vaseline while he was gone and now they're both slick as ice on an asphalt road in the middle of winter."

He started laughing again.

"I swear, Rand, I'm not going to protect you if Max comes after you." Elizabeth smacked him on the arm for good measure then turned to Kaitland. "The children think it's a game, as you can tell, and no one can get them out."

"Oh, dear," Kaitland said. She clasped her hands together, trying to decide what to do. "Move away from the bed, Max," she finally said.

"But…" He looked to where the children were, then back to Kaitland. Without another word, he slid his arm from under the bed and moved away.

Kaitland grabbed a blanket and lay down on the floor. She turned her head to where the children were. Max, Rand and Elizabeth, plus all the staff, were staring at her as if she'd lost her mind, but she ignored them. "Well, there you are, my two little termagants," she said sweetly. "Hi there."

Two little stark-naked babies, their eyes round, stared back at her. "Peekaboo," Kaitland said, and shot a grin to both kids.

Maddie clapped.

Bobby chortled.

Kaitland took the blanket and eased it up over her eyes, then jerked it down again. "Peekaboo," she called out again.

Maddie squealed and wiggled around in the small space.

Kaitland lifted the blanket twice more then dropped it, eliciting responses from both children.

"I don't see what—"

Kaitland cut Max off with a wave of her hand. She finally pulled the blanket up and left it over her face. There was the expected chortle, clapping, then another squeal. Then the sounds changed, to demanding.

Finally, Max said, "Well, I'll be..."

Kaitland felt two hands jerk on the blanket. "Pee-boo!"

She wrapped the blanket around Maddie. "Pee-boo yourself," she said, grinning and hugging her close.

Max quickly wrapped another blanket around Bobby.

"Let's get them washed up and then we'll have that bed blocked so they can't get back underneath."

"Amen to that," Max said. He touched his hair with disgust. "At least it'll wash out of the clothes I have on."

Kaitland looked at the cotton pants and light blue top he wore. As usual, he was gorgeous. Not even a little Vaseline could detract from that. She reached up and slicked his hair back. "There. You look fine now."

"He looks like James Dean," Rand commented.

"Well, maybe I just like the James Dean look," Elizabeth said and walked over to Max. Bussing him on the cheek, she said, "You have much patience. I don't know how you put up with him."

"Long-suffering, that's what I am," Max said, grinning superiorly at Rand.

Rand snagged his wife. "Come on. I think we need to have a talk about just who you're suppose to be loyal to."

Elizabeth giggled, winked at Kaitland and Max and left with her husband. Seconds later they heard a squeal, a giggle then absolute quiet.

Kaitland glanced at Max and cleared her throat.

Max smiled. "I like Rand's way of getting her loyalty. Lead the way," he added. "Let's get these two monsters cleaned up."

They put the children in the bathtub and began to scrub them. "You're amazing with children, Kaitland," Max said as they soaped up each child.

Kaitland shrugged. "You will be, too. I've had years of practice, don't forget. This is all new to you. With time, everything will come to you."

"I don't know. I was so angry and frustrated. I only walked out for a couple of minutes to go retrieve an outfit from the other room. I couldn't get to these two. I kept thinking, if they can get undressed and into trouble that fast, what if something serious happens? What would I do then? Would it mean their lives because I was inattentive?"

"Oh, Max," Kaitland murmured. She washed Maddie's hair, ignoring the splashing. "Don't say that. Children are children. I sometimes think it's in their nature to explore and get into mischief. You'll learn that things like this are just going to happen. It's not something to get upset over. Save getting upset for the other dangers they'll drag you through, not the minor things."

"I don't consider this minor," he said.

"By tomorrow you will. Or when you realize you could have moved the bed to get them."

Max's shock was priceless.

"Careful what you say," she warned.

He decided against saying anything.

"Of course, they would have still played catch-me-if-you-can if you'd moved the bed. It would have probably taken two of you, one on each side, to catch them. And it wouldn't have been as entertaining to Rand."

Max sighed, then a reluctant chuckle slipped out. "I imagine I looked pretty silly."

"You reminded me of one of those kids on the black-and-white TV shows that wore his hair straight up. It was pretty comical-looking."

"Gee, thanks."

He wrapped a towel around Bobby and stood. Going into the other room, he dried the boy off and automatically dressed him. "I've already lost an hour's worth of work up here with these two."

"Which you can do later," Kaitland said.

"Yeah. I never realized how nice it is to be able to work out of your home. I go to the office three days a week and the other two days my secretary works on what I give her. Then, of course, on the weekend I go through our company's local stores. I imagine I'll have to make three or four trips a year to the other apparel stores as things come up," he told her. "However, I'm thinking on expanding Dugan's job from head of security at our store to problem solver. The man is brilliant. He's a former cop who enjoys a challenge. If I brought him on full-time, he could be the one going from store to store, trouble-shooting for me and then I'd make the decisions. That way I could be with the children more until they're older. I'd only have to make a couple of trips a year, with Rand only making a couple, too.''

Dressed, Bobby jumped down from the bed and toddled over to the toys. He pulled out colored plastic blocks and began to bang them together.

Kaitland, done with Maddie, patted the little girl's bottom and sent her off toward Bobby. ''Have you heard anything about the adoption proceedings?''

''The lawyers are filing the papers. It'll be a little longer before everything is settled. They warned me, though, that negative publicity could really hurt the case, especially since I'm single and already have such a bad reputation thanks to the newspapers. What's so disgusting is that the reputation is false, but it just doesn't matter. Maybe my mother was right to want...'' He glanced at her, then away.

He sat down next to Kaitland on the bed, then reached out and took her hand. Tracing the back of her fingers, he asked, ''So, how'd it go today? Any press catch up with you?''

Kaitland shivered at his touch. Forcing her voice out, she replied as calmly as possible. ''No. They haven't figured out who I am, yet, I don't think.''

''I'm sorry about this. I'm usually so careful. I won't tolerate the children's chance at adoption being hurt by this. I've set wheels in motion for retractions.''

His hand continued to stroke hers. Kaitland watched, mesmerized at the sight of his darker skin against her lighter tone. His hands were neat, clean, his fingers long and slim.

She raised her gaze to find him staring at her.

Her heart fluttered at his concerned, almost wary look. Suddenly she wanted to tell him everything. She could tell he was thinking about the incident five years ago. But she was afraid he would hate her when she told him the truth. She was so ashamed. Logically, she knew it wasn't her fault. But there was that small part that told her if she hadn't gone to that room, answered that note...it wouldn't have happened.

"Actually," she said, fear rising in her. "I think I'd like a kiss. That might help me forget about today." *And the other, too,* she added silently.

She leaned forward and placed her lips against his. His kiss was gentle, yet reserved. She could feel it as if he had said it out loud: I can't release myself to you until I know what you did.

She tried to deepen the kiss, desperate for only a moment to forget the past. Max's hands rose. He gently disengaged himself from her. Definite concern was etched on his features. "What is it, Kaitland? Tell me."

A scream pierced the room.

Kaitland and Max both jumped and whirled. Maddie was covered with blood, holding her head. Bobby held a metal jack-in-the box in his hands. "Oh my goodness!" Kaitland cried, jumping up.

She ran over to Maddie and scooped her up. A cut about a half an inch long slashed across her head. It was deep enough that it would need stitches. "Max?" she called.

Max, who had Bobby and looked almost as white as the paint on the wall, came over to her, shushing Bobby as he bounced him. "Is it bad? Look at all the blood."

"She'll live. But this is one of those times I told you about earlier. She's gonna have to go to the hospital and have stitches."

"I'll get Darlene to stay with Bobby and then we'll go."

He headed toward the door with Bobby. While he

explained the situation to Darlene, Kaitland found a cloth to press against Maddie's head, then grabbed the diaper bag.

Downstairs, as they were getting in the car, Max totally surprised Kaitland with his attention to priorities. Instead of worrying about the leather upholstery of his car getting stained, he strapped Kaitland in, because she was holding Maddie in her arms, and said, "Just take care of my little angel there, and we'll worry about everything else later."

He went around the car and climbed in and Phil shot off toward the hospital emergency room.

Kaitland held Maddie close, rocking the child who was now only sniffling. She was relieved that she'd been given a reprieve from telling Max about the incident. But she wondered now if it wouldn't have been better just to get it out and deal with his shock rather than wait until another opportunity arose. *Dear Father, help me make a decision. Give me the courage to do what is right.*

Chapter Eighteen

"So, what's the trouble?" Rand asked, walking into the study where Max was sitting.

Max glanced up at his brother. "Home early today, aren't you?"

Rand shrugged. "I had a feeling."

Those feelings they shared. Max wasn't surprised Rand had picked up on this. He sighed, tossed down the reports he was working on, opened a drawer and pulled out a plain manila envelope. Tossing it onto the desk, he waited for Rand to pick it up.

He watched Rand slide out the pictures. His mouth tightened. "These are new. Same incident, just different poses."

Max's gut clenched. "Yeah, I noticed."

Something in his tone must have alerted Rand to how he was feeling. His gaze shot up to lock with Max's. "How serious is it between you two now?"

Max sighed. "I never stopped loving her. I realize that now. I don't know when the realization came, maybe seeing her with the children, or hearing her laugh, or just having her around where I couldn't hide behind other things. But it's still there.''

''Along with the hurt.''

''Yeah. Along with the hurt. She almost told me the other day. I mean, call me perverse, but I just have to hear why she decided to cheat on me. Maybe if I hear the reason, I can get on with my life.''

''What about your feelings?''

Max shrugged. ''We don't choose who we love. But we do choose who we forgive. I can't completely let this go until she tells me where I failed.''

''Where you failed?'' Rand looked at him oddly and Max knew he was wondering what he meant.

Rand hadn't heard the final fight between their parents. He'd never shared that one thing with Rand. How his mother had accused their father of failing to protect her and the children from the press. How she wanted a divorce. Max's father had insisted they take a vacation to get away from it all…and then they had died. His mother hadn't been able to handle the pressure of the family's notoriety, the fast rise her husband had made in the business world. And his father had failed their mother. It reminded him too much of his situation with Kaitland and how afraid he was that he was going to fail her or that she would get tired and leave. That was his real fear. Maybe she had gotten tired of seeing reports about his alleged romances and decided to prove something to him. But that was something he would not discuss with anyone. He never had and never would.

''Maybe she failed?''

Max shook his head. ''I only know I love her.''

Rand shifted the pictures, then frowned when he came to the note.

"They want a pretty penny for these," Rand murmured, scanning the note. "Or they'll release them to the press."

Slipping everything back into the folder, he passed it to Max. "What are you going to do?"

Max liked that about Rand. In important matters, he didn't try to force his will on him, he treated Max as an equal. Rand was the best friend he had. And he needed to discuss things with him, knowing it would go no further, knowing he wouldn't be condemned for any decision he made. "I don't want Kaitland hurt."

"If these pictures hit the stand, you know they'll ruin her career at the day care."

"Jake knows about this incident," Max told him. "But you're right. Being splashed across the front page, being exposed to the public eye in such an intimate position, even if Kaitland and the senator are completely clothed, would be a guilty sentence. But I won't pay hush money. There's never a good ending if you do that."

"There's something else bothering you, isn't there?" Rand asked.

"I'm worried about how this turn of events is going to affect the adoption of Maddie and Bobby."

Rand leaned back in his chair and crossed his legs. He wore a business suit and conservative silk tie. His hair was slightly rumpled after a full day at work. He rubbed his eyes, which meant his contacts were bothering him. He usually came home and changed to glasses. But instead, he'd come straight to his brother.

"I don't know what to tell you, bro. The evidence is incriminating."

He sighed, saw Max's stricken look and shook his head, disgusted with the situation.

"Kaitland will probably lose her job at the day care," Max said. "She's also primary foster parent for the kids right now, though I should receive approval in the next day or so. Still, the church's board of directors would probably take a dim view of the publicity the media would generate when that was also found out."

"And we know the media will do anything for a story, they would, of course, exploit this state of affairs no matter how loving and caring Kaitland is," Rand added. "If the outcry is loud enough, it could very well affect the outcome of the adoption. And here's something we haven't thought of before. What will the senator do when these come out?"

"Do you think he's being blackmailed too?"

Rand shrugged. "If he is, I doubt he'd tell us. Maybe the best thing to do is to contact the police at this point. I admit, when things happened years ago, you were too upset to deal with it. But for it to come back now...to torment you twice. This guy is a treacherous blackmailer. He's not going to go away. Unless he's caught, this is going to hang over you and Kaitland for the rest of your lives."

"Isn't that just the truth," Max muttered.

"You know, if it's any help, there's a verse in Psalms that tells us not to worry about the world, that our enemies will soon wither. God takes care of His own. Maybe you just need to pray and leave it in His hands. Let Him guide your next actions."

"Yeah. I've been praying. All day, on and off. But I fear that something is going to happen to the kids—"

"They're resilient," Rand interrupted. "Sometimes we have to go through a few trials so that we're strengthened."

"Like Katie and me?" Max asked, knowing his brother.

"Yeah. Kaitland wasn't ready to marry you five years ago. You weren't really ready to marry, either. You've both grown, been through some hard times. Your love is deeper now."

"Are you saying I was shallow?" Max asked, surprised.

"No. But weren't we both just a little naive, living in our own world, thinking we controlled everything that went on around us?"

Max was astonished at how open Rand was being with him. He realized something else, too. "You're right. We were pretty arrogant back then. The great Stevens empire. No troubles, the world loved us, everything was going smoothly."

"Pride goes before the fall," Rand added.

"And fall we both have." Max relaxed, peace flooding him. "And now God is restoring."

Rand's eyes widened at Max's meaning. Then he smiled. "Let me know when you convince Katie of that."

That was the first time Rand had ever called Kaitland by her nickname. He knew now she would always be a part of their family. "Well, learn patience, brother," he said as he shoved the paper back into the desk. "She'll have to come to some decisions herself and we still have to work out what happened five years ago."

"You'll do it," Rand told him. "We'll all be here for both of you. But you're gonna have to trust her, Max."

"I do, basically." Max said.

Rand shook his head. "Let go of the pain before it ruins your newfound love. Then pop the question." He stood. "Let me know what you decide about that." He nodded toward the closed drawer. "Now I've got to go find my wife. I've been home too long without telling Elizabeth hello."

"Did I hear my name?" Elizabeth said, breezing into the room, her purse on her shoulder.

"Uh-oh," Max said, leaning back in the chair and watching Rand's smile drop.

"You're not going out, are you?" Rand said.

Elizabeth chuckled, leaned forward and slid her arms around Rand's waist. "And hello to you, too. You're not due home for at least three more hours." She nuzzled his neck, placing a trail of kisses there until she reached his mouth.

Max felt sorry for Rand. He looked disconcerted, trying to concentrate on what he'd asked her, and deal with the havoc his wife was playing on his senses. "Stop that," Rand finally muttered. "You'd drive a sane man crazy."

She laughed again, her smile lighting her eyes. Rand's features immediately softened. "I'm worried, honey. Tell me you're going right back upstairs to rest."

"Oh, Rand," Elizabeth said, attempting a pout, then giving up when it didn't work. "Why did the…"

"And no jokes," he warned.

Max knew how she used jokes to distract as well as make them all look foolish. It was the latter she'd probably been about to try on Rand. And Rand was unable to withstand her jokes. He was learning to cut her off early before she could reduce him to a pile of mush.

She shrugged. "My friend Laurel is meeting me for a late lunch."

"But your pregnancy…"

"Is perfectly normal," she said, taking his hand and placing it on her abdomen.

Max felt suddenly out of place. He shifted in his chair, thinking of how he'd have felt had it been Kaitland who had almost been killed.

"Maybe Rand is right," he offered.

Both of them looked at him incredulously. "Hey, I can side with my brother once in a while," he added defensively.

"Traitor," Elizabeth muttered. Turning back to Rand, she said, "You know Laurel was off freelancing for some newspaper when I was working for you. She arrived back just in time for our marriage and then we went on our honeymoon—it seems almost six months since I've seen my dear friend."

"We've only been married..."

"I know how long we've been married. I said it only seemed like six months because I didn't have much time when we planned the wedding. I'll be back in an hour or so. She and I have a lot to catch up on. Besides, she's the one who called me! She asked if I'd be available today at this time to talk."

Rand rolled his eyes. "You should be resting."

"Trust God to keep that which has been firmly planted right where it should be," she said softly, earnestly.

Max saw his brother sinking to that pile of mush again and knew Rand was lost.

"Be careful," Rand muttered, looking as if he couldn't figure out how he'd ended up giving her his blessing. "Call me if you need me. And take your pager with you."

Elizabeth squealed happily. "You're such a teddy bear," she said and hugged him.

She gave him a kiss and was out the door in a flash before Rand could change his mind.

"Teddy bear?" Max asked, his voice reeking with laughter.

Rand actually flushed. "She has these crazy names. And I don't want to hear them from your mouth again, little brother, or we'll have to take it outside."

Max's eyes widened as if to say, *who me?* "Teddy bear..."

The phone rang.

"Answer that," Rand said and strode out of the office.

"Hello?"

"This is Marjorie Wiscott calling for Kaitland Summerville."

"I'm sorry, she's not in right now. May I take a message?" *Marjorie. Marjorie? Where did he know that name from?*

"Just have her call me, please, when she gets in. It's about a story for the local paper."

Max's blood turned cold. "Thank you." But the woman had already disconnected.

Marjorie Wiscott. Yeah, he knew the name. He'd seen her byline several times, she'd written about his family in the newspapers here. What in the world was she doing calling Kaitland and what story was she talking about?

"Hi, Max. I just wanted to let you know we're back."

As if thinking about her had summoned her there, Kaitland came striding in the door, wearing a tailored pink shirt tucked into loose gray trousers. A slim belt around her waist and loafers, both dark, completed her ensemble. She looked like a poster for middle-class motherhood.

He looked in her eyes, trying to see any reflection of pain or bitterness that might send her to a newspaper. It wasn't there.

"What's the matter?" she asked, hesitating near the chair.

He waved her to be seated. "Tell me, Katie, are you still angry at me? Would you be willing to betray me again to get revenge?"

He could have slapped her and caused less pain, if the look on her face was any indication. But after that call...

"I'm not running this time, Max. I'm trying to stay here, prove to you that we can put the past behind us." Kaitland dropped her head. "I never explained, just turned my back on everything years ago. I realize how wrong that was now."

"Katie, che'rie," Max said softly, standing and coming around the desk, his anger over Marjorie falling away. "I didn't ask you for an explanation, either. We were both hurting and yet I was arrogant enough to expect you to say you were sorry. You might say we were both at fault."

"I didn't see it that way," Kaitland whispered.

"Nor did I," Max admitted. "I don't know why you betrayed our trust, or why you suddenly found my touch so repulsive, but I know now I should have tried harder to work things out." But he knew part of the reason he hadn't tried. Part of that fear...that dark monster that ate at him, the one he'd never let go of years ago, after his parents' deaths.

"Oh, Max," Kaitland replied, her pain in her eyes. "Please don't blame yourself."

"How can I not when those children up there could be ours now if I'd only tried harder with you."

Tears filled Kaitland's eyes. "It wasn't that easy. We both had to grow."

"You sound like Rand." Max finally accepted that Kaitland wouldn't betray him again. He was almost certain of it. Rand had told him to let go of his bitterness. Until that call, he hadn't realized how much pain was still stored up inside him. *Father, forgive me,* he prayed. He just had to let go or he was going to be eaten alive.

But that call. Why would the woman call here as if she knew Kaitland?

"I always thought he was a smart person." Kaitland smiled, her eyes meeting his.

"Don't tell him that, he'll get an ego."

"He already has an ego," she said.

He just couldn't let go completely, he realized. That one small part of him remembered the photos and the betrayal, as well as the call. He had to ask. Maybe soon he would be able to trust her. He'd even thought maybe he had started to, but that call... "Do you know a Marjorie Wiscott?"

Kaitland stiffened.

The hopeful part in Max withered at the suddenly shuttered expression on her face. *No, God. Please, not again.*

"I've met her a few times."

He felt it starting all over again. He'd been ready to confess his love, and now this. There had to be an explanation, he told himself. Maybe she likes the woman and isn't ever offended by anything the press says. If he pushed it, maybe this time things could be explained. And if she decided to marry into the family, maybe she wouldn't eventually get tired of what the press tried to do to her to leave. "She called here for you a few minutes ago, about a story."

He watched her closely. Her eyes widened, then she sighed. "I'd hoped to tell you before anyone else got a hold of you..."

"What?" he asked, anger seeping into him. "Katie, you know how I hate the press. What does Marjorie want? She's one of the people who has written stories about my family in the past. Why was she calling here for you?"

"You know, Max, you're going to have to get over your aversion to the press. Not all journalists are total jerks that would sell their souls for a good byline."

"But Marjorie is," he replied, remembering some of her stories.

"No. She wouldn't sell her soul. But she would buy a story. And she would pursue one too. She found out I asked for an additional week of leave from the day care. I thought it would give you a little more time to get your license as an emergency foster parent and a little more time for the furor of the rag magazine's story to cool down before I went back to work."

Max felt bad. "I'm sorry, Kaitland. I didn't realize. I didn't think about that. I bet you're in hot water over this at the day care. I want to apologize for not thinking about the press following us to the fast-food place."

"It's no big deal." But he could tell by her eyes that it was a big deal, as was his doubting her. She sighed, then smiled. "And no. I'm not in hot water. Jake was concerned. He wasn't angry, he was dismayed that I was taking an additional week. But you have bigger problems to worry about. You see, I found the perfect way to appease Jake's dismay about my additional week of leave. As of today, you're going to have to look for a new secretary.''

Confused, Max asked, ''What does Jennifer have to do with this situation in the press and Jake and u…and everything?'' He wasn't going to say *and us.*

''She's the new assistant day-care director at the church. I needed some help. She loves kids. I approached her. Did you know she once owned a day care?''

''Jennifer?'' He was still lost. Kaitland had the ability to do that to him.

''Yes. She had to close the day care because of her mother's death. Actually, it was her mother's business. But I think Jennifer will be wonderful working for Jake.''

''You stole my secretary.'' It was beginning to sink in. She really wasn't worried about the story in the press. He'd hurt her, but instead of dwelling on his blundering mistake, she was going on to something else.

''I'm also paying her better than you are.''

''When is she leaving?'' he asked, astounded, and just a little touched by Kaitland's ability to go on despite the circumstances. She was strong. She wasn't a weak person. It made him wonder if he had been wrong about five years ago. Could there have been an explanation other than the obvious one? Could his Kaitland have actually been innocent in it all? Could the pictures have lied? She was too strong to let herself get messed up in such a situation unless she had been behind a deliberate attempt to hurt him and to extort money from him.

''Two weeks. She's going to give you her notice tomorrow. And be nice to her.''

"I wouldn't be anything but nice," Max replied, indignant. "I guess if Jennifer's leaving means things will be easier for you at the day care, as well as here, with the kids, it's okay."

She smiled. "Good," she said as she stood.

Max felt bereft. "Katie?" He stepped forward and took her hand.

Startled, she looked up at him. He didn't know what to say. So many questions whirled in his mind. He rubbed his hand over her fingers, gently, back and forth. "Your hand is so soft."

She smiled, her features softening. "I want you, too, Max."

He leaned forward, touching her lips to his. When she didn't resist, he dropped her hand and wrapped his arms around her. He felt her own arms wrap hesitantly around him, then she was returning the kiss. Her lips were soft, yielding, seeking warmth and comfort. He gave what he could and accepted what she freely gave.

Finally, he lifted his head. He leaned against his desk, pulling her more securely against him and dropping his head on top of her soft honey blond hair. "I just don't know what to do, what to believe."

"I want to tell you, Max…" He waited. Her voice was so weak, vulnerable, that it actually sent chills up his spine. "I can't stand the ultimate rejection again. I just couldn't go through that. It hurt too much the first time."

He realized it was his fault that Kaitland sounded so defenseless. He was at fault because in a way, he had betrayed her own feelings all those years ago by not staying and confronting the problem. And because he still didn't trust her, was afraid of what he'd hear, he still might hurt her again. "I want to know, Katie. When you feel up to telling me."

The spell was broken. With his words, she pulled back. A sad smile touched her lips and her eyes reflected years of pain that he'd never realized she felt. His gut twisted at the sight. "I just can't," she told him. "Not until I know you won't turn your back on me."

He stared helplessly. "I want to say I'd never do that, Katie."

"But you did, five years ago."

He nodded wearily. "I did, to my great regret."

She turned and headed toward the door. "You know, Max," she said as she paused at the entrance. "I never stopped loving you."

He watched her walk out and knew he couldn't concentrate on work now. All he could see was that sad resignation in Kaitland's eyes. And he knew, somehow, that he had put that look there. And it scared him to death.

Chapter Nineteen

"**I** think you'd better sit down."

Max turned from where he'd been staring out the window to see his brother striding into the room. His face wore a thunderous expression and he clutched a newspaper in his hand.

"What? What is it?" Max asked, coming forward.

Max's surprise evidently registered with Rand, for he slowed, and actually held the paper back. "I'm sorry, Max. I didn't mean to startle you. I just wanted to get here before anyone else."

It was six-thirty in the morning. Max knew the paper had only been delivered, just after six. "What is it you're trying to tell me without telling me?" he asked, seating himself on the sofa and waiting for Rand to do the same.

He didn't. He stood in front of Max with a look of regret on his face.

For the first time, real alarm grabbed Max in the gut. He'd seen that look on his brother's face before...always when bearing bad news. Slowly, feeling as if his arm was made of lead, he lifted it toward the paper.

Rand hesitated again, then finally handed over the paper. "Front page of the State section."

Max opened the paper to that section...and sucked in his breath at what he saw. Instant Daddy, the headline read. A picture of him lifting Maddie into his arms at the fast-food restaurant was underneath the headline.

"'Max Stevens as he lifts his soon-to-be daughter into his arms,'" he read under the photo.

His glance jerked up to Rand's, whom he realized recognized the implications. Who knew he was adopting these children? A few pictures in a rag magazine was one thing. But someone close to him had given this story to the state paper. They wouldn't have printed it otherwise. And with such accurate details.

He felt sick at the implications. "'Bachelor or Daddy or both,'" Max read the article out loud. "'Our local celebrity, the most eligible bachelor in the tristate area, who has done an admirable job of matching wits and avoiding the matrimonial knot, has finally met his match in a set of twins that were left on his doorstep just a month earlier. According to sources, the twins, Maxwell Robert and Madeline Renée were deserted on multimillionaire Max Stevens's doorstep with a note asking him to take care of them. And that he has done, falling head over heels in love with the two small cherubs, insofar as he has decided to adopt them as his own...'"

Max let the paper drop. He was going to be sick.

"Maybe it was someone else, Max. There's no proof it was Kaitland."

Max looked up bleakly. "The byline is Marjorie Wiscott's." He paused, then added, "The same woman who called five days ago to talk to Kaitland about a *story*.''

Rand ran a hand through his hair, pushing at his glasses because he hadn't had time to put in his contacts, then finally sighed. "I can't understand why she'd do this. She knew how you felt about keeping this information out of the newspaper, didn't she?"

"Oh, yeah, she knew," Max said, even though his heart felt as though it were shattering into pieces at his feet. "I told her exactly how I felt. But she just seems to do things over and over like this, doesn't she?"

"Who does things over and over?" Kaitland asked, strolling into the room with Maddie in one arm. The cut on the little girl's head had completely healed. Kaitland gave Max a smile. "Darlene has Bobby and we're heading for breakfast. I thought you might..." She trailed off and frowned at Max's expression.

Rand was frowning, too. "I'll leave you two alone," he said, refused to meet Kaitland's eyes and walked out.

"What's the matter, Max? What's up?"

Kaitland was concerned. She'd never seen Max look quite so stricken, except...

The blood left her face. "You're scaring me, Max. What is it?" She sank into a chair, releasing Maddie who was wiggling. In the background she could hear Bobby and noted Maddie took off at a toddle for her brother's voice. She thought to stop her, but the slap of the paper in front of Kaitland froze her to the spot.

The picture stood out like snow in a jungle. But what was even worse was the headline and what the article said.

Total silence greeted her when she was done reading. She didn't want to look up. Feelings of that time so long ago mixed with feelings now. Dread, fear, nausea. It was happening all over again. The silent accusation in his eyes had said it all.

She started to stand. She would leave, go up to her room and give Max time to think this through. As she'd told Max a few days earlier, she couldn't go through the pain again.

"Why, Katie?" he asked, his voice full of anger and confusion. "You knew how I felt about those children being exploited. You aren't cruel enough to have done it for revenge. And I know you don't tend toward gossip. So, that only leaves the money. But I offered you money to help pay your grandmother's bills. So, why would you go to a stranger and sell her a story only you know? It's just like five years ago. Questions but no answers. Your actions are that of a malicious, conniving money-grubber. I didn't want to believe it five years ago...nor when I started receiving these." He opened his desk drawer and pulled out a manila envelope. Pouring out the contents, he let the pictures fall in front of her.

Pictures of her and the senator spilled out. Dizziness engulfed her. "But what am I to think when I get blackmail notes both last time and this time when you are in my house? Not a single one the entire time you were gone. But as soon as you return..."

Blackmail notes?

He'd been getting blackmail notes and pictures? Strangely, she thought, she was relieved. Maybe then, the picture she'd inadvertently seen on his desk that day had been one of these. Yes, there it was. She saw it now, partially covered by another one. At least he hadn't been holding on to it and using it to remind himself of what she'd supposedly done years ago. Yes, that was a relief, wasn't it?

Max didn't wait for her to comment. He only swiped a hand through his hair and continued, "I just don't understand your game, but I'm tired of playing, Kaitland. I won't risk my feelings anymore and then end up with the heartache you dish out."

"How do you know it's me who leaked the story?" she said feebly, thinking to argue the article.

"Marjorie's byline. Are you going to tell me it wasn't you?"

Looking at the condemnation in his eyes, Kaitland finally gave up. What was the use? He'd never really forgiven her for five years ago. She'd known, on some deep level, that he hadn't and that's why she'd always been afraid to tell him what had happened.

And if she argued now—his mind was set against her. "No, Max. I'm not telling you it wasn't me."

She had to get out of here, out of this house, now! "Darlene is quite competent at handling the children," she told him. "Please send someone with my things."

"What do you mean?" Max demanded, standing, too.

"I'm quitting. Effective immediately. I'm sure you don't want a conniving—what was it? Manipulating…no, malicious, wasn't it? Yes, malicious, conniving money-grubber. I'm sure you don't want that kind of person in your house any longer. Heaven forbid, she might steal the china, or the strongbox you keep unlocked in your drawer."

At his surprised look, she nodded. "Oh, yes, remember, you once showed it to me—before." She started toward the door. "You know, Max, I was a fool. I had prayed and thought God had opened this door so we could work things out and go on with our lives. But I see you don't want to go on. You want to harbor that hurt and nurse it and baby it so it never goes away. You'll never learn, will you? I would say you're going to be hurt over this when the truth comes out...but just like five years ago, it probably won't come out—the truth, that is. So, Max, have a nice life. Stay hurt, and buried in your fears and insecurities.''

She turned at the door and faced him. "I'm tired of trying. I'm closing the chapter on this part of my life and going onward. Goodbye, Max." .

She walked out, past Rand who was holding one of the children with Darlene, past Timms, the butler, out the door to her car. The only thing in her car were the keys, since they always left the keys in their cars. Her clothes, her purse, everything, was still up in her room. But she didn't care. She would take no more of Max's pain. She had to get out, go away where she could lick her wounds. For, as she'd told Max, she gave up. She would not try anymore.

"Father, help me," she whispered, starting her car and driving down the driveway. "Just help me get the car home in one piece before I fall apart."

Chapter Twenty

The sound of the front door brought Kaitland's head up. She'd been lying on her bed for almost an hour, crying until her nose was stopped up and her throat raw. For some reason, she hadn't thought she could hurt again the way she had hurt the last time.

She'd found out she was wrong. Uncurling from the pillow she clutched, she moved her Bible to the side and stood. Only one person entered her house without her permission.

Her brother.

Just what she needed to top off a disastrous morning.

"I see by your face you saw the paper this morning. Or rather, your ex-fiancé has," Robert said, stomping into the living room. "Who ran the article—you or him? Well, that was a great way to thwart any blackmail," he continued, confusing Kaitland.

She rubbed the tissue across her nose. "What are you talking about? No. I don't want to know. Look, Robert. I really don't want company right now. Can't this wait until later?"

"If you want Max to lose those two little brats he's trying to adopt, then by all means throw me out," he sneered.

"That's ridiculous. You have no control over that. Why are you so angry?" Her head was beginning to throb. She just didn't have the patience for Robert today.

Robert raised a haughty eyebrow. "Are you willing to risk that?"

Kaitland sighed. It did no good to argue with her brother. He was totally self-centered. If he thought he needed something, he would go to whatever lengths possible to get it. If she threw him out, he'd only rant and rave for the next month until she finally listened to what he had to say. "Fifteen minutes. That's all you get."

She only wanted to go back into her room and crawl under the covers and cry. She had three more days before anyone would expect to see her at church. She could hide and pray and cry until some of the pain left and the numbness set in and then she could start to function again.

"I need some help at a function in two days and I want you to do it."

She stared at him, dumbfounded. "Do I look like I'm in any condition to go to one of those parties?" she asked, unable to believe how callous her brother was. "Besides, I've told you before, I don't like those events. What makes you think I'm going to change my mind now?"

"Those children."

"You're not going to get some senator or someone to help you against Max. Come off it, Robert. And your power doesn't extend past there."

"It will eventually. And you're going to help me. Why not take a look inside this envelope here."

Kaitland picked it up and dropped into a chair near her dining-room table. Nothing could be worse than what she'd been through this morning. It was simply easier to go along, then when Robert was done asking, tell him no. Opening the envelope, she shook the contents into her lap, and gasped when pictures of herself and the senator were revealed.

Her stomach churned but she managed to keep her voice steady. "Max already knows about these."

So, someone had told Robert about this, too. Her whole life was going to end up on the front page pretty soon and she didn't have any idea who had taken these pictures.

Max's words came back—his accusatory tone. No, it wasn't someone Max had hired, though she had wondered at one time. Could he have been so jealous as to take the pictures? She knew better now. Then the senator maybe? No. She'd been over this hundreds of times in the last few years and had come up with a hundred different people, but had discarded each one. Who could it have been?

"I know that," Robert said scathingly. "You lost your fiancé because of these. You wouldn't have been happy with him. He'd keep you up there in their house like some princess and never let you out again. You wouldn't be able to work or enjoy life. You wouldn't be able to help me anymore or even be my sister. He'd see to that."

"You've talked to Max about these pictures?" she asked, not understanding what he meant by his statement about losing Max. How could he have known that so fast...unless he'd gone by the house? Oh, no, she thought miserably. No wonder he was so angry.

"Not exactly, Kaitland. I'm the one who gave Max those pictures."

"But how did you get them?" she asked, then realization dawned. Kaitland thought she was going to be sick. She was wrong. The day could get worse.

Pain tore through her heart and her eyes filled with fresh tears that she refused to let fall. She gulped in a breath, forcing the bile back down her throat.

"You set me up." Her voice was barely audible over the roaring in her ears. Black spots danced before her eyes and her head spun crazily. A hard jerk on her arm, the biting pain from Robert's fingers, brought her back from the brink of darkness.

"You're my brother. How could you?" Her heart was bleeding pain as she stared at the man whom she had always loved like a blood brother.

"Come on, Kaitland. I was never really your brother. Your grandmother made sure of that."

"That's not true. You were always my brother to me. Grandmother just wanted you to be a little reasonable."

"No. Your grandmother wanted me to be more like her family than my family, whom she told me several times was below your family's lineage. She always thought your mother married beneath her family. And whether you realize it or not, she didn't want me near you. She said I was a bad influence."

Kaitland wondered if that was true. She couldn't remember her grandmother being that way. But that wasn't the issue. "So, that's what my grandmother might have done. But why take out your anger on me?'' she asked, her voice sounding weak to her own ears.

Robert shook his head. Finally he said, "You don't get it, do you? This isn't about you. This is about power. I want power so no one will ever have control over me again. I was desperate with the senator. I had to get something on him because he wouldn't listen to reason on a bill that was coming up. I knew you wouldn't let him under your skirt. But maybe just a few pictures of him with you might do the trick—and they did. Both of you fell for the notes so easily.''

"You've been playing some sick game with my life?'' She remembered the pain of the past five years and couldn't believe her own brother—no, her *step*-brother—had done this to her.

"You're going to help me again,'' he said, not answering her. "I need some more pictures of a couple of different men. I'm losing some of my power over various committees in the state senate and I've got to get these guys in compromising situations. You don't look the part of vixen and would be perfect for my scheme.''

"You can't seriously believe I would help you. You're crazy.'' Rage was boiling in her. She could feel herself beginning to tremble over how this person had destroyed her life.

"Oh, am I? Well, let me share a little fact with you. Those two kids Max loves so much just happen to be mine.''

Kaitland laughed, albeit a little hysterically. "Well, you've certainly kept them a secret if that's so.''

Robert shot her an ugly look. "Those pictures of you worked wonders with the senator. But you refused to go to any more dinners with me. I had finally found a way to get to some of these men. They all have families, and whether it's their actions or that they're lured there, none of them could explain pictures away. I found someone else who would help me. But Samantha got pregnant.''

Kaitland felt sick again and her hysteria was instantly cured. She knew that was the name of the children's mother. She remembered Max telling her that. With clarity she realized that Robert was telling the truth. ''Bobby,'' she whispered, remembering that Maxwell Robert was Bobby's real name.

''That's right, sister. They're mine. However, Samantha ran off in the middle of the night. As I couldn't use her when she was pregnant, I decided to find someone else. But I haven't been able to find anyone I really trust. I'm desperate. Some of the men don't believe I'm a formidable foe because the ones I bribed are gone from office. I need more pictures. And if you don't help me, I think I might just have to claim those brats.''

''I won't do it, Robert!'' she said fiercely. ''You know I won't.''

''It's your choice. You keep going back to this Stevens jerk. Fine. You want to marry him, go ahead, but you're gonna have to do this for me first,'' Robert said. ''It's critical I get at least this one senator in a situation. Senator Bradley is against gambling. If I don't find something on him, he's going to sway some of the others to ban gambling in this state. I have too much invested in a gambling venture to let that happen. Once I control him, some of these other conservative bills he's been pushing will be under my control, too.''

''What's to stop you from claiming the children anyway?''

''What's to stop me from sending these pictures to

the newspaper and ruining Max's chance in a custody suit when it comes out what type of person he has allowed to take care of his wards? Just think what that would do to his very family-oriented business. Or what it would do to you, too, not to mention those kids, who I will then immediately claim and of course get custody over. I can just see the court when I explain that Samantha ran off without telling me and that when I saw today's story, I realized I'd finally found my children.''

''You don't even care about Samantha, do you?''

He shrugged. ''I saw the kids that day at the house. They looked like Samantha. I hired a detective and found out she was dead. She was too clingy anyway.''

Kaitland stood, despite how shaky her legs were and went to the door. She pushed it open, using its solid strength to hold her up.

''You make me leave without an answer and I'll ruin your boyfriend.''

''Do your best,'' she replied coldly. ''He and I are not involved.''

''What about the kids?'' he asked, his shock evident, though he tried to hide it behind bravado.

''Go for it,'' she replied only after a slight hesitation. ''Just leave now, Robert, and don't come back. It's going to take me a lot of prayer before I can ever face you again.''

He sneered as he walked past her. ''Fine. Don't help me. I'll find someone to do the job before Saturday. But let me tell you, Kaitland. You're gonna be sorry you didn't help. Those kids sure did mean a lot to Max.''

He sauntered out. Kaitland knew it was because he thought he'd struck a nerve. And he had.

As soon as he was out of sight, Kaitland rushed into

the bathroom and threw up, until there was nothing left in her. Then she lay against the tile floor and cried.

"Father, what do I do now? This is all such a mess. I don't want him touching those kids. I'm so angry I think I honestly hate him at this moment. How could he have turned out this way?"

But she knew. Just as Saul, who had been called by God and anointed king, had turned his back on God and sought out a soothsayer for his guidance and assurance, so had her stepbrother turned his back on God and had been given over to a reprobate mind.

"I can't think about him, Father. It hurts too much. You work on him and change him," she begged. "I don't want to see him. I can't help him anymore or even be a friend to him. And I can't let him take those children. Or hurt another senator. What am I going to do?"

An idea came to her. She realized there was really only one thing she could do. But to do it was going to require more courage than she had shown in the last five years. She was going to have to walk right back into the lion's den and deal with one of the Stevens brothers.

"Just don't let him eat me up and spit me out when I face him, Father," she said.

She rose and washed her face and prepared to face Rand Stevens at the headquarters of Stevens Inc.

Chapter Twenty-One

"Who let you in here? Get out. Now!"

Rand looked like an avenging angel when he was mad. And boy was he mad. He had been sitting bent over his desk looking at some papers when she'd managed to sneak past the secretary. She'd told the woman she was waiting for Max and they would go in together when he arrived. As soon as the secretary had left her station, she'd slunk in.

Now Rand stood, pushing up his sleeves as if he was getting ready for a fight. She'd never known Rand to be physical, but he scared her just the same. She backed up against the door. "I'm not leaving until I tell you what I came to say."

"You'll leave right now." He came forward, striding across the carpet like an angry lion about to pounce.

She turned her head, closed her eyes and gritted her teeth, pushing her hands against the door and digging in her heels. This had been a stupid idea. She knew Rand and Max were close, had remembered Max saying Rand had taken her side years ago, but of course, she hadn't seen him right after the incident. He was going to throw her out of the office—physically.

When nothing happened, she opened one eye and peeked at him. He stood a foot away, staring at her strangely. "You know I'd never hurt you, Kaitland. God knows I'd like to throttle you right now for what you've put Max through, but I wouldn't physically assault you. So stop cringing like that."

"Well, the way you came after me gave me my doubts," she replied hesitantly, not moving from her position.

He sighed. "It's Elizabeth. She never gives an inch. I forget how intimidating I can be." As if realizing he had relaxed, he stiffened. "You have exactly five minutes to tell me whatever you think is important."

She sagged against the door. Where to start? She was so relieved, her mind went blank. Overload of all that had happened today, she was sure.

"Well?" Rand asked, but his voice had softened. He hesitated only a moment before coming forward and taking her by the elbow. "You look like you're about to fall down. Come over here."

That one act of kindness was her undoing. She burst into tears—again. Embarrassed, she tried to keep her face down where he couldn't see, though she was wailing loud enough that Max's secretary could probably hear her in the other wing of the building.

She felt a hesitant pat on her head, then her shoulder, heard a grumbled statement and then she was hauled into Rand's arms. "Okay, che'rie, take it easy. Cry it out and then tell me what's the matter."

"I love Max!" she blubbered through loud wails of distress.

"You have quite a way of showing it."

She slapped his chest, which caused a grunt from him. "Ah, all women, they are the same," he murmured, his accent thickening, so much like Max's. "You have the same spirit as my Elizabeth when she's ready to pull my hair out. I do not envy Max," he said. "Now tell me. Why did you go to the press?"

She cried another five minutes before she was able to talk. "I'm s-sorry," she stuttered, sniffling loud and blowing her nose. "I had to tell you. The senator. Jonathan Bradley, your friend, only an acquaintance of mine," she said in disjointed sentences. "It's my brother. He's behind it. You need to tell him. I love him."

"I know you love your brother, but let's go back..."

"Not my brother," she cried. "*Your* brother. I love him. I hate my brother." She paused. "Well, I don't hate him, but I really want to at the moment. He's ruined my life."

"And the senator?"

"He's gonna ruin his life," she said.

Rand sighed. He released Kaitland and stood. Going over to a small bar area, he poured her a glass of ice water and wet a cool cloth. "Wipe your face," he said when he returned to where she sat. "Drink this, and we'll try again."

She did as she was told. "Now, che'rie, tell me what is the matter," he said as he resumed his seat next to her.

"I told you."

He looked as if he was getting upset. "Do you mind if I ask a few questions?"

Realizing she was still making a muddle of her explanation, she nodded.

"What is this about Senator Bradley being your brother?"

Kaitland's eyes widened. "I didn't say that."

"Then what did you say?"

"Senator Bradley is on a committee about gambling. You know Robert does some heavy lobbying. He's known as a man who can get the job done. Or he was. Evidently, he's losing some power in his reputation. He wanted me to help him with Senator Bradley. I had to do what happened before—lure Jonathan to a room and then let Robert snap pictures of me and the senator in a compromising position. I couldn't do it. I refused, but he's going to find someone who will do it and I knew you were friends with Jonathan and he wouldn't believe me since we are only passing acquaintances and it *is* my brother…"

Rand had stiffened and his face turned thunderous. "Your brother was the one who took the pictures? Then you and he *have* been trying to blackmail Max."

"No!" Kaitland cried. "You see, I was almost raped—" She gasped.

Rand's eyes sharpened and focused on her.

"Oh, please," she whispered, almost moaning in shame. "Please don't tell Max."

She dropped her head and began to weep softly. *"Juste ciel,"* Rand said softly in French.

Good heavens. She'd heard Max say the expression enough times.

"I think I am beginning to see, che'rie. Tell me then, if I am mistaken. You were in that room with Senator Richardson without knowing what was about to happen? Your brother took pictures. He used them to break up you and Max. You held your tongue because you love your brother."

"No." She shook her head, negating his words. Taking a deep shuddering breath, she whispered, "I'm so sorry. I'm not usually so emotional. I just feel as if I've lost everyone in the short span of three hours. I didn't know until today that it was my brother who had taken those pictures. He told me, at the same time he threatened to take the children from Max."

Rand sat up. "Maddie and Bobby? How?"

"Oh, Rand. That's one of the reasons I'm here. I'm no longer speaking to my brother. As I tried to explain a moment ago, Robert wanted me to lure Jonathan Bradley up to a room and help him get incriminating photos on the senator. I refused. He told me that Maddie and Bobby are his children. He was using the threat of taking them back, as well as exposing those pictures, as leverage. I told him I didn't care about my reputation. I plan to resign from the day care, of course, so he can't hurt the church. But I won't let him use the children, or hurt Senator Bradley." She paused for a moment, then, "There has got to be something you can do to protect the children and help the senator. Robert plans to tell the authorities that he has been searching for the children's mother and the story this morning led him to them."

"This would have been a lot easier if you hadn't gone to the press with the story."

"I didn't."

Rand looked at her in shock. "Then who did?"

She shrugged. "I have no idea. It's true Marjorie Wiscott and I are on-again off-again friends. But she never interviewed me for this story. I know it's under her byline. I plan to call her later and find out where she got her information. I'm not sure she'll tell me, if the person who gave it to her asked to be anonymous.

All you have to know is it wasn't me. I'm not the source.''

Rand studied her, then he looked grim. "Max is never going to forgive himself for this. Nor am I likely to forgive myself. Forgive me, che'rie, for not coming to you and finding out the truth. You have been through more than you should have had to go through."

Kaitland's shoulders slumped. "It doesn't matter, Rand. I had hoped Max loved me enough to forget the past. I just couldn't confess to him…" She trailed off.

"He wouldn't have blamed you," Rand said softly.

"Five years ago, he tried me and judged me without an explanation, Rand. And did it again. He would have blamed me. Please don't tell him about the incident I mentioned. Let him believe what he wants. It's better than him knowing my secrets and then rejecting me…or worse, apologizing out of guilt."

"You misjudge my brother. You're right—he should have forgiven you instead of holding on to the pain and keeping it close to his heart. But we aren't perfect. Sometimes it's easier to hold on to it than risk our hearts again. It's wrong. God tells us to forgive *and* forget. We cannot forgive and then make the person pay a penance for their mistake. However, that's what we often do…and if not them, then ourselves.''

Kaitland was jolted by his words and looked up into Rand's understanding eyes.

"Forgive yourself, Kaitland," he said. "Let God heal your heart. You did nothing wrong five years ago except not come to my brother and explain. This is the same thing you have done today. I will tell you, Max will find this out and will come to you to hear the truth. You must stop hiding behind your walls and confess all.''

"He'll pity me," she whispered. "And probably feel guilty."

"Good. A nice dose of guilt should help clear his mind, make him stop pitying himself." He smiled at Kaitland. "If nothing comes of it between you two, then that's fine. But at least you will again be able to live and go on and you will be stronger, as will my stubborn-headed brother."

She chuckled. "That's what he thinks of you."

Rand chucked her under the chin. "He's wrong. I'm happily married and very biddable now." He stood. "Go home. Rest and pray. I'll make sure Jonathan knows what's going on. And I'll make sure Robert can't get the children."

At the pain in her eyes, Rand added softly, "I know your heart must be breaking over what you must do to your brother. But you're doing the right thing. Let God wrap you in peace, che'rie."

She nodded. "Please don't tell Max about..." She looked him in the eye. "About what happened five years ago."

"It's not my story to tell. When he comes to you, you will tell him."

She thanked him and left, keeping her head down so no one could see she'd been crying. As she walked to the elevators, she thought it unlikely Rand would be right this time. She was certain Max wouldn't ever darken her door again. But Rand had been right about one thing...she was doing the right thing. No matter how much her heart felt as if it was being ripped out, she couldn't let Robert hurt someone else.

Chapter Twenty-Two

"We need to talk—again," Rand said, going into Max's study.

Max looked up and met his gaze. "You said that once. I don't care to hear it again."

"You may look like a wreck at the moment, but I can guarantee you, Kaitland looks worse."

"Kaitland? When did you see her?" Max's eyes widened in shock and in them was a hint of wariness mixed with hope.

Rand shook his head in disgust. "What is it with you, Max? I love you, but you're so mule-headed stubborn. Why have you ostracized Kaitland so thoroughly without finding out what was going on?"

"She's the one who went to the paper. I should have known..." He trailed off and shook his head.

Rand strode forward. "What, Max? What should you have known? I never bought that you just broke it off with her. You're the type to be easygoing with most things, but I could tell you cared for Kaitland. When this fiasco happened five years ago you ran from it, I would say it was in relief, if I didn't know better. And now, again, a newspaper article and you just let her go once more. There's something more behind this and I'm not letting you get away without telling me this time.''

Max glared at his brother. ''It's none of your business.''

Rand walked over to the desk, slammed his hands down on it and leaned forward, scowling. ''It is when my own flesh and blood is tearing himself up over it. What is it? What should you have known? Tell me!''

Max erupted. ''I should have known she was just like our mother.''

Rand's eyes widened, then he nodded with understanding. ''I never realized you knew, too,'' he said and sank down wearily into a chair. Max sank down too as if his outburst had exhausted him. ''Why didn't you ever mention to me, in all of these years, that you knew of our mother's betrayal? Especially when Carolyn died in a car accident?''

Max shook his head. ''I know it sounds crazy, but there were so many times I'd wondered if we drove her to leave Dad. We were such a handful. Had she not been leaving him, he wouldn't have insisted on one last vacation alone so they could try and work things out, and they both wouldn't have died together.''

''Oh, Max,'' Rand said. ''It's been so long.''

Max shrugged. ''Dad loved Mom. Too much. He should have let her go and he would be alive. They both would. He wanted her too much.''

''And you think that's the problem here? That Kaitland is going to find she doesn't like the life of the rich and famous like Mom and ask for a divorce? Or is it that you're afraid of loving her too much and chasing after her like Dad chased after Mom,'' Rand said with dawning realization.

Rand shot out of the chair and began to pace. ''I have heard some stupid things in my life…but fearing you love Kaitland too much takes the cake. You would rather let her go than risk loving her? You would rather make her absolutely miserable than go after her.''

''But with Kaitland it's different. She did betray me before we were married and again with the reporter. Are you suggesting I actually go after someone like that? No matter how much I love her, I'd be a fool if I did.''

''You're a fool if you don't,'' Rand told him. ''You're so busy trying to find some way she might leave you like Mom tried to leave Dad so you can prove to yourself that you shouldn't love her that you've missed out on the one person who loves you more than life itself.''

''Just what do you now about it?'' Max demanded.

''I know she didn't betray you with those pictures.''

''How do you know?''

Rand scowled. ''You'll have to ask her. I promised not to say anything. But I can tell you she didn't betray you with that article, either.''

''She told you that, too.''

''Yeah. And if you weren't so bullheaded, you'd figure that out just by knowing Katie. And I know she didn't break off all contact with her brother and come to me to tell me he was going to try to get the kids—his kids—away from you because she just happens to be planning to try some other way to hurt you.''

Max fell back into his chair, shock on his face. ''She did what? Maddie and Bobby are…*pooyah-ee!*'' His *good grief* came out in French he was so agitated.

"I'm afraid so," Rand said. "I have our lawyers on it. I just came by to tell you that you've made a major mistake with Kaitland and if you let it go this time without fixing things, I'm afraid I'll have to take you outside and beat the stuffing out of you."

Max blinked. "You and what army?" he asked, his own temper finally sparking at the way Rand was treating him.

"It'll only take me. Because when you figure out everything that has transpired, you'll feel too guilty to fight back."

Max sought for a hole in Rand's argument. "If you're so sure Kaitland wasn't the source for the article in the newspaper, who was? It had to be someone who knew our family inside out. That information could only have come from someone in here, and if you tell me Timms, Sarah or Phil did it, I'll laugh."

"It's my fault."

Rand and Max turned to stare at the door where Elizabeth stood looking absolutely awful over the situation. A newspaper was clutched in her hands.

"What are you talking about?" Rand asked, going over and gently taking Elizabeth's elbow and guiding her to a chair.

"Stop treating me like an invalid, Rand." Then, turning to her brother-in-law, "Oh, Max, I'm so sorry. I had no idea until I got the paper about fifteen minutes ago. I slept in this morning because I wasn't feeling well. When my friend Laurel called me the other day, it was because she wanted to interview me. I didn't realize she wanted an official interview. She has this instant-recall memory so she doesn't use tape recorders like most people. However, she asked me what was going on...we go so far back I didn't think anything of it. We laughed and joked. When I saw the article this morning, I knew what had happened. She sold the article to Marjorie Wiscott who had approached her about it. She thought it would be fun done as a tongue-in-cheek, which she said she's no good at writing. And I have to admit the article is like that. But she thought I had given my permission for the article. I've never been so shocked or embarrassed in my life. I'm so sorry," she repeated. "I'm planning to go over and tell Kaitland immediately it was my fault... Max? Are you all right?"

Max moaned and dropped his head to the desk. "Please leave. Both of you," he whispered, his mistake so glaringly obvious that he couldn't stand to face anyone.

"Max?"

"Come on, Elizabeth," Rand said. "Give him time."

He heard both of them leave, heard them pull the door closed behind him. When no one was around, he allowed his grief to pour out.

"Rand was right. Why have I held on to the hurt and pain all of these years? Why couldn't I accept Kaitland for what she was, a gentle soul who loved me? *Loved me.*" He pounded his fist on the desk again, his misery obvious. "Loved, as in past tense. There is no way she could have cared for me. At least, Father, that's what I thought. How could she love me? My mother was so unhappy that last year of her life. She didn't like being in the spotlight. She hated it. I just knew Kaitland would hate it and would pull some crazy stunt like my mother did to try to break off the marriage. Of course, my mother's crazy stunts had been just disappearing for a week or two at a time, telling my dad she needed time away, until that last time when she told Dad she wanted a divorce. I just knew Kaitland wasn't the type for the limelight. She's so quiet, gentle, kind and loving. She reminds me of a flower, so fragile.''

He stood and walked over to the chair where he knelt and dropped his head to his arms. ''But she's not the one who's in the wrong. She's never been in the wrong. I've run her off both times. I've wronged her more than anyone deserves. What a fool I've been. What am I going to do?''

He continued to pour out his heart until the pain lessened and God finally restored a peace that had been missing from his life for many years, a peace that passes all understanding.

And he knew what he had to do.

Chapter Twenty-Three

"We got him."

"Jonathan?" Kaitland asked. She hadn't talked to Jonathan in over six months. "Senator Bradley?"

"Yes, Kaitland. It's me. The police told me the part you played in helping me. I appreciate that, though I wish it would have proven unnecessary. However, I called to thank you and tell you personally that Robert had a woman approach me Saturday. He came with the *evidence* today that the undercover policewoman he solicited helped him acquire. The circle is completed and he was arrested. If it helps, he actually looked resigned to what had happened. I think there might be hope for eventually reforming him."

Kaitland sighed. "Only with God's help. He has so much anger in him. But I appreciate your call."

"I wish it hadn't been over such circumstances," the senator said. "However, now that I have you on the phone, I remember about six months ago you promised one day you might take me up on my offer of a date. I have something special planned, a nice quiet dinner at my house tonight. Only two or three friends. Do you think you could fill in as my date?"

She had thought Jonathan wouldn't remember that or their few meetings at different functions. She was wrong. And she was wrong about how forgiving this man was, too, if he could ask out Robert's sister. "Oh, Jonathan, I don't think so. I really don't feel up to it."

"It's important, Kaitland. I know we're not very close as acquaintances. I won't pressure you that way. I know you've been through a difficult time."

"News travels fast."

"Indeed it does. But please, consider coming over to my place at seven. Like I said, I wouldn't ask if I really didn't need this. Consider it me collecting on an old debt."

"I would think, Senator, that my information could serve as that," she said warningly.

He sighed. "You're right. Then I might as well give you a hint. It's about Max. If you won't do it for me, then would you come for Max and the kids?"

Kaitland dropped her head in defeat. She'd only met Senator Bradley a dozen times. They weren't intimate friends the way she and Jake or Shirley were or even Jennifer, with whom she had become close in the past few weeks. But all he had to do was mention Max's name... "I shouldn't, Senator. But I'll come. I'll stay for exactly one hour and then make an excuse. If you haven't told me what you need by then, I'm gone. And you understand I'm only doing this for Max?"

That husky voice of his rumbled across the lines. "Oh, yeah, sweetheart. I definitely hear that. See you then."

He hung up.

Kaitland immediately called herself ten kinds of

fool. She should have refused. Max was a closed subject on her life. Today had been her first day at the day care and everyone was treating her as if she were made of spun glass. It was driving her crazy—maybe because that was exactly how she was feeling. She'd actually agreed to go to Jonathan's house so she could tell everyone tomorrow she'd gone out on a date with one of the most handsome and eligible men in Baton Rouge—next to Max, of course. That would shut them up and hopefully stop their looks of fear and pity whenever she walked past.

Going upstairs she decided to take a quick shower and then determine what to wear. Something cute and flashy—the exact opposite of what she was feeling. She would wow them tonight, even if she didn't feel as though she could wow poison ivy at the moment.

"Senator Bradley," she greeted, walking in, glancing around curiously. She'd never been to Jonathan's house before. She was impressed. It was very nice, low-key, conservative just like the man, though it hinted at money in its simplicity.

"Let me take your wrap."

She looked up at Jonathan. He was taller than Max, probably six-two. His light hair and tanned skin glowed from the lighting in the other room. His green eyes were twinkling and his lips twitched with a smile. She turned and allowed him her wrap.

"Are your other guests here yet?" she queried, clutching her purse.

He gave her another one of those quirky smiles and nodded. "They're on the terrace. I have a few things I need to do. Won't you please go on out and… introduce…yourself." He motioned her ahead of him

toward the living room. Across the way she could see
a dimly lit patio that led to gardens beyond.

She hated this. She absolutely hated this. "About
Max?" she said, wanting to find out why he had insisted on her presence.

"Later," he replied and headed down the side hall,
leaving her standing in the living room.

Her emerald green dress was long, slit up the side
to her knee and sat just off the shoulders. Small flashes
of silver glitter sparkled on the material.

She'd coiled her hair up in a French twist and carried
a small purse that she could hold in one hand, hoping
to feel sophisticated.

All she felt was foolish.

She didn't want to socialize with people she didn't
know. But if this was about the children and Max...

Taking a deep breath, she walked outside, thinking
the party must be farther in the gardens. She hesitated
just through the door.

The night was crisp, cool, and the smell of flowers
wafted to her on the air. Stars shone, just coming out
as it was twilight. Patio furniture, very nice wood with
cushioned seats, was scattered around in an artful dis-
play of disarray. It was dark enough that at first she
didn't notice the shadow off to her left near one of the
paths through the jungle of gardens.

Something, though, must have alerted her to his
nearness because she stiffened and searched the area
until she located the shadow. As if sensing another person's presence, the shadow straightened and turned.

Her heart began to hammer against her chest.
"Max?" she whispered, uncertain if her eyes were
playing tricks on her. Unconsciously, she took a step
back, her purse falling from numb fingers.

The figure froze.

"Max?" she asked louder.

A squeal to her right forced her head around and she saw Maddie and Bobby toddling up the path with Darlene. When the children spotted her, they let go of their nanny and lunged toward her.

"Maddie up!" the little girl demanded, thrusting her hands up toward Kaitland.

In shock, unsure what to do, she responded automatically. She lifted Maddie into her arms and bussed her on the cheek, wiping off the extra lipstick, tears filling her eyes when Maddie gave her a very sloppy kiss back.

"Me. Me! Me!" Bobby demanded and she awkwardly bent and scooped up Bobby, too.

"They missed you," Max said.

Pain lanced her heart and she trembled at his voice. She kissed Bobby, who immediately pushed her face away and began playing with the earring in her left ear. She chuckled, though it was a very unsteady sound. "I missed them, too," she said. What did he want? Why was he here? She would have sworn he wouldn't have anything to do with her again. Yet here he was, staring at her with those deep dark eyes, revealing nothing of what he felt. How odd. With Max, she pretty much always knew what he felt. He was very open and vocal. Or at least he had been with her.

Maddie immediately wiggled, wanting down. Bobby, of course, followed his sister. "Darlene, Jonathan said milk and cookies were waiting for them inside."

Darlene immediately herded the children toward the prize. A small smile touched Kaitland's mouth as Maddie and Bobby jabbered on about cookies while eagerly toddling through the doors.

"So, where are the other guests?" Kaitland asked, looking around in expectation once the children were gone.

"There are no other guests, che'rie." His voice was soft, husky, deep with feeling.

No. She couldn't handle this now. Not today. She was still too raw from everything that had happened this last week. "You asked Jonathan to call and set this up, didn't you?" she accused, eyeing the door with longing.

"I thought we should meet on neutral ground. Please don't go," he added when she turned to do just that.

She froze. Max never begged. But it sounded as though he was pleading right now. Without turning around, she asked, "What do you want?"

"I want to know what happened five years ago."

Bitter pain twisted inside her. "You know. I betrayed you. Remember the pictures." She was trembling so badly she knew if she took a step on these heels she would fall off. But which would be better? Making a fool of herself running away or breaking down in front of him? He didn't give her a choice as he stepped into her line of sight, inadvertently blocking the exit.

"I know there were pictures of you taken. But you're not that way, Kaitland. You're too gentle to ever do something so underhand."

"Oh? And what finally convinced you of that?" she sneered, furious suddenly that this topic was about to be dredged up again.

"I think I always knew the truth. But as my brother pointed out today...*juste ciel*, it wasn't you, Kaitland.

It was never you. It was me. I just couldn't accept that you might not get tired of my way of life. I was looking for an excuse. And I found it in spades with those pictures.''

Kaitland felt unexpected tears overflow at the pain in his voice.

He continued, ''I found a lot more than I was expecting in those pictures. And *oui, che'rie,* I was hurt. But I held on to my pain instead of letting it go like I should. I held it in my heart. Instead of forgiving you and forgetting like the Bible commands, I harbored the pain and allowed it to grow, using it as proof that you would one day leave me like my mother...''

He stopped.

His mother? Max had never been insecure. At least, she'd never known him to be insecure. Seeing a dawning light in what had only been a dark void before, she asked a question that would continue what she had thought a hopeless subject. ''What about your mother?''

Pain darkened his gaze, his eyes making her heart break. She watched as, instead of facing her, he turned and stared off into the sky as if contemplating the origin of the stars. ''My mother was very unhappy the last two or three years of my parents' marriage. She didn't like the media and what they were doing to our family. My dad kept telling us that publicity would help the store and just to ignore all the erroneous things that were published. But she couldn't handle the way they exploited us. I can remember many times finding her crying. I never told Rand, never shared that with him. It's the only thing I've ever kept from him. But I swore if I ever married, I'd find a woman who didn't mind publicity and I would make sure my children were protected from the barbs and things the media threw out. And then I met you, and fell in love with you. But you were so soft, tender, innocent, I knew the press would eat you alive if they ever sank their claws in you. I knew you'd be unhappy and would eventually leave.''

''You sure didn't have much confidence in my love, did you?''

He shrugged, still avoiding her gaze. ''It wasn't that. I guess I never got over the way my father fell apart that last year as he tried to convince my mother to stay and the nightmare of my brother and I being left to our own devices when we had been such a strong family up until then. I was afraid to risk it with children. So, it wasn't so much that I didn't trust you as I didn't trust marriage. I love you, che'rie. More than life itself. I only realized during prayer, after I'd run you off a second time, what an absolute fool I've been, not allowing God to heal my pain and trust Him to see us through to the end.''

He held out his hand. ''I won't do again what I did five years ago. I wanted to come to you and find out just what happened. No more hiding behind walls. No more running. If our love is to last, we must be honest—no matter what.''

Kaitland's knees knocked together. She couldn't reach out, afraid she was going to faint at his words. *Be honest—no matter what.* Well, what did it matter? How much worse could it get? Unable to stand still, she went over to a path and started down it. She could hear Max by her side, but refused to look at him. If he touched her now, she would finish the crying jag she had started at his confession. Instead, she inhaled the fragrance of azaleas and honeysuckle as she walked.

And she remembered.

"The party I went to five years ago was really something," she said finally. "I've been to plenty of parties, but this one was different. It was just before Mardi Gras and the women's gowns seemed more glittery than normal, the men more jovial. The people there had had a good year and were in the mood for celebrating. Of course, I enjoyed how outgoing and friendly the guests were since I tend to shy away from situations where I have to talk. However, I'm still the old Kaitland and prefer to have someone I know by my side even if someone else is doing all the talking. That's why I never minded going to parties with you, Max. The people at those functions are low-key, they're polite and you never leave my side."

She sighed, a lonely broken sound that echoed loudly in the garden. "That's why, when my brother, Robert, disappeared and then I got a note asking me to come to his room, I assumed it was from Robert."

"It wasn't Robert?" Max asked.

"Oh, yes, it was. But the note to the senator was from him, too."

"I don't understand. Why would your brother do that? Why did he want you there?" Max asked. "Your own brother?"

Kaitland shuddered. "Yes. My own stepbrother. He's the one who set up the senator to get some pictures of him in a compromising situation so that Senator Richardson would have to vote Robert's way. He's also the one who, because of his note and stupid plan, almost got me raped."

Tears started.

Max didn't force her to explain more, just reached out and pulled her into his arms and held her as she cried for what had happened, for their own disaster and for all of her disillusionments in the past few hours. And as he held her, he murmured words of love and soft soothing sounds, stroking her back, her hair, her arms.

All the while rage ate at him. Rage at what her step-brother had let occur, rage that she had held this in and rage that he had been such a thrice-cursed fool and not insisted on finding out the entire story when it happened. Because of him, his Katie had suffered untold sorrow and had had no one to turn to for help. *Ah, Father, help me. Forgive me for my excessive foolishness,* he prayed.

Kaitland clung to him and cried until there was nothing left in her, then she collapsed against him.

He pulled out a white silk handkerchief and fluttered it in front of her face. "Well, che'rie, it looks as if the children aren't the only ones to ruin my suits. However, you, I don't mind."

She sniffled again, a pitiful sound on the cool night air. Wiping her face, she tried to move back.

"No, che'rie. I'm not letting you out of my grasp this time. I was more than an idiot last time not to ask you. However, *ma petite,* I'll hear it all."

Never had his accent been so strong. She knew how much he was hurting for him to lapse into his own language. Her heart cried out for the pain of it and the new pain she would cause him with the explanation. "Don't blame yourself, Max. I didn't try to stop you when you turned your back on me. I'll tell you though, I never stopped loving you. I couldn't, though I was tempted to try after the newspaper article appeared."

Running her hand down his shirt, she stroked his chest in comfort. He tightened his arms around her.

"That was Elizabeth's fault, che'rie, for which she has profusely apologized. Just one more sin to add to my list," he muttered.

"No, Max. Never. God forgives. He forgets. I forgive you. And I will forget. I want you to forget, too, never again to condemn yourself for your mistakes. Because what I'm asking of you now is forgiveness in what I am going to share with you."

She shuddered. "My stepbrother has never felt as if he was accepted by me or my grandmother, so he feels no blood tie. Even though we aren't blood-related, I've always considered him my real brother."

Until now could have been added easily, the way Kaitland paused after that statement.

"He has this unhealthy need for control," she continued. "Evidently, as long as he has control, he has power over other people, and he feels superior. His greed knows no end. More power, more control. By getting into lobbying like he is—was," she corrected, "he was able to feed that need for power. But it wasn't enough. He couldn't make people do what he wanted..."

"Until now."

"Right. That's why he lured me up to the bedroom where Senator Richardson thought I was waiting for him. He snapped a few shots, threatened the senator and then he had that man's votes."

"He's not a Christian, sweetheart," Max said simply. "And he has a lot of bitterness in him. I'll talk to him and make sure he understands he's not to bother you again or I'll bring additional charges against him."

"For bothering his sister?"

"No, che'rie. For trying to blackmail money out of me. Those pictures you saw me with that day and the ones I've received since were sent with a note threatening me if I didn't do what he wants.''

"But that would hurt your reputation."

"Who cares? Maybe once I worried about the paper. But I let the fear of what the press would do to my eventual family consume me so much that I ruined our chances before we could start. They can print what they want as long as you promise never to leave me over the erroneous things that will crop up.''

"I haven't left you yet and look at all the lies they've printed about you so far? Including,'' she added, a small smile in your voice, ''that you just got back from Colorado where you were secretly meeting with a certain European princess who was there on vacation.''

He chuckled. "I had forgotten about that story that happened when Rand was in therapy with Elizabeth. Of course, it was quite a shock, coming back to find my brother had regained his sight. So, it's understandable that I forgot about that one.''

"My point,'' Kaitland said, "is that the stories have never bothered me. That's how these magazines are. They thrive on sensationalism. And it's good for business,'' she teased before sobering when she pulled back and met his gaze. ''I'll confess now that I didn't come to you years ago because I was ashamed of what had happened. I was afraid you'd look at me differently. Please forgive me for that.''

He shook his head. ''Never would I look at you differently, che'rie. And of course you're forgiven. As you said, God forgives. He forgets. And starting today, after the harsh lesson we have both learned, I promise you I'll do my best never to look back on a wrong but to forget it and go forward. Nothing else matters but that I love you, Katie. I want you in my life the rest of my days. I love you, and I need you. The children love you and need you. And I wouldn't be averse to adding a few little ones to the brood, either. We can forgive the past, accept the lesson we have learned from it and look forward if you're willing.'' Max reached into his pocket and pulled out a small box.

Kaitland accepted it from his hands, opening it reverently.

Inside was nestled an emerald and diamond ring. ''Oh, Max,'' she whispered.

''It's the same as the necklace and earrings I bought you years ago.''

Looking up, she asked, ''You kept this all these years, even though you believed I'd betrayed you?''

Max shrugged. ''Despite what an idiot I was, I never could let you go.''

Kaitland smiled, her luminous eyes shining from the tears there. ''I guess I was right when I felt it was God prompting me to take the job.''

She held up the box and held up her hand. Max readily slipped the ring onto her third finger. She stared at it, murmuring, ''God has certainly worked out many problems between us and cleared up so many questions I had about the past.''

She lifted her hands and placed them on his shoulders. Looking into his eyes, she allowed her regret to show. ''I'm sorry, my love, I didn't come to you sooner and ask forgiveness for my stubbornness. I have no excuse. I used my hurt to hide behind, thinking you were the one who should have come forward.''

Max stroked her cheek, gently tracing the curve of her delicate bones. ''God works on His own timetable. As Rand said, neither one of us were probably ready five years ago. And remember. *Forget.* It is over, to be remembered no more. I'm ready to go forward with the certainty that God is leading us and guiding us and will protect our steps every day of our lives. How about you?''

Kaitland stared up into the dark brown eyes brimming with love and promise. Her heart swelled to overflowing with her love for this man. ''Oh, yes, my love. I'm more than ready. Ready to take you on, the kids, and your obnoxious brother.''

Max laughed huskily. His eyes, though, burned with his love. ''That's the spirit. And you're gonna need it if, as my wife, you're going to help me keep Rand from corrupting those two little termagants.''

Kaitland's heart lifted, soaring to the heavens.

''But first, let me do something that has been long overdue.'' Max leaned forward and placed a loving kiss on her lips, pulling her into his arms. She reveled in the sweetness as he molded her lips to his, consuming her with his tenderness and yes, love, with no inhibitions between them. Her fingers slipped into his silky hair and she stroked his neck, her heart almost beating itself right out of her chest.

Finally, he lifted his head. Kaitland rested in his strong arms, allowing him to hold her weight against him. Slowly, she lifted heavy eyelids. ''That is what you wanted to show me?'' she asked, confused though pleased.

''That,'' he replied, grinning very smugly at her reaction, ''and my promise to cover you with those each night for the rest of our lives.''

He lowered his head and their lips met again, this time with a promise of bright things and the future ahead.

* * * * * *

Acknowledgments

Wow. A second book. And so many people to thank. My GEnie pals, Kathi Nance, Judy DiCiano, Shannon Lewis and Nancy aka Igor; and Yvonne Grapes, my mail critique partner. And Gayle Anderson who willingly read over the manuscript for mistakes. They are wonderful to bounce ideas off of.

And of course, Jean Price, my agent, and Anne, my editor, who have been unfailingly patient with me as I learn the process of what goes into publishing a book. And Anita Slusher and Debbie Weaver.

But most of all, my daughter, Christina, my son, Jeremiah, and my husband, Steve, who are so wonderful about eating spaghetti or leftovers when I'm at the computer.

Dear Reader,

Ideas come from many places. I love baby stories and I love twin stories. And I like happy endings. When I started Max's story, I thought about how we sometimes are urged to forgive, but it's so often only lip service. "I'll forgive you. But you're gonna have to really earn back my trust. And it's gonna take time!" And yet that goes against what the Bible teaches us. God tells us to be like Him. Forgive and forget. *Forget* being the word we usually leave out! I thought, wouldn't it be nice to see a story about a man who fears the pain from his past and is betrayed on top of this. We see him gun-shy, yet not so sure just how badly he wants to love. So, he professes forgiveness, but hangs on to the memory of the pain—until God points out the error of his ways. And of course, I always like the humorous things children get into, considering I have two of my own and always have a brood over. I hope you enjoy Max's story of tenderness and triumph. Not just with Katie, but with those two little lively angels that are left on his doorstep. Write me and let me know. P.O. Box 207, Slaughter, LA 70777.

Yours truly,

Cheryl Wolverton

Continuing in April from
Love Inspired...

FAITH, HOPE & CHARITY

a series by

LOIS RICHER

Faith, Hope & Charity: Three close friends who find joy in doing the Lord's work...and playing matchmaker to members of this close-knit North Dakota town.

You enjoyed the romantic surprises in:

FAITHFULLY YOURS
January '98

Now the matchmaking fun continues in:

A HOPEFUL HEART
April '98

Faith, Hope and Charity are up to the challenge when a headstrong heroine clashes with an impossibly handsome lawyer. Could love be on the horizon?

And coming soon, a dedicated nurse falls for the town's newest doctor in:

SWEET CHARITY
July '98

IFHC2

This April...
Love Inspired invites you to experience the
work of one of America's best-loved writers...

Carole Gift Page

This talented author of over thirty-five novels
returns to Love Inspired with

DECIDEDLY MARRIED

When a couple's marriage is put to the test, they
must find the strength to renew their commitment
to each other—and to God.

After nearly twenty years of marriage, Julie Ryan
didn't want to admit that her marriage was in jeopardy.
But when her devoted husband, Michael, revealed that he
felt emotionally distanced from her, she had no choice but
to face the truth about herself, her relationship to the man
she loved—and her faith in the Lord. And when a family
crisis arises, will this troubled couple find the courage
to confront the future...together?

**Don't miss this tender story about the
resilience of love...available in April from**

ICGP398

Available in March from

Love Inspired...

Child of Her Heart

by

IRENE
BRAND

The author of over fifteen inspirational romances,
Irene Brand brings Love Inspired readers a
heartwarming and emotional story.

Pregnant and alone, Sonya Dixon faced the biggest
challenge of her life. But with the Lord's help and the
love of the right man, Sonya just might have the
family she's always dreamed of.

Watch for **CHILD OF HER HEART** in March
from Love Inspired.

IBRAND

This March watch for the next story about the lives
and loves of the residents of Duncan, Oklahoma,
as *Love Inspired* brings you another

by
Arlene
James

EVERYDAY
MIRACLES

Every day brings new challenges for young
Reverend Bolton Charles and his congregation.
But together they are sure to gain the strength to
overcome all obstacles—and find love along the way!

You've enjoyed these wonderful stories:

THE PERFECT WEDDING
(September 1997)

AN OLD-FASHIONED LOVE
(November 1997)

A WIFE WORTH WAITING FOR
(January 1998)

Now meet Parker Sugarman, a bachelor who
desperately wants to keep custody of his orphaned
niece. But Parker needs a wife, and so proposes
marriage to his good friend Kendra. He knows she'll
be a wonderful mother. But will Kendra's faith be
strong enough to help Parker become the perfect
family man? Look for:

WITH BABY IN MIND
available in March from

Love Inspired

IEM98-3

Welcome to *Love Inspired* ™

A brand-new series of contemporary inspirational love stories.

Join men and women as they learn valuable lessons about facing the challenges of today's world and about life, love and faith.

Look for the following April 1998
Love Inspired™ titles:

DECIDEDLY MARRIED
by Carole Gift Page

A HOPEFUL HEART
by Lois Richer

HOMECOMING
by Carolyne Aarsen

Available in retail outlets in March 1998.

LIFT YOUR SPIRITS AND GLADDEN YOUR HEART
with *Love Inspired!* ™

Steeple
Hill™

LI498

Welcome to *Love Inspired*™

A brand-new series of contemporary inspirational love stories.

Join men and women as they learn valuable lessons about facing the challenges of today's world and about life, love and faith.

Look for the following March 1998 Love Inspired™ titles:

CHILD OF HER HEART
by Irene Brand

A FATHER'S LOVE
by Cheryl Wolverton

WITH BABY IN MIND
by Arlene James

Available in retail outlets in February 1998.

LIFT YOUR SPIRITS AND GLADDEN YOUR HEART

with *Love Inspired!*™

Steeple Hill™

LI398